CAPE MAY BEACH DAYS

CLAUDIA VANCE

CHAPTER ONE

The wind whipped Sarah's hair while she stood at the front of the pontoon boat as it glided over the water, picking up speed. She smiled, closed her eyes, and took a deep breath, inhaling the fresh, salty marsh air. Some other boats whizzed by, their passengers waving, and to their left and right, along the wetlands, were a variety of the shorebirds they'd come to watch.

The boat pulled up close to a spot that granted an excellent view of some osprey nests on manmade nesting platforms. Sarah squinted to get a better look when she suddenly felt a hand on her shoulder.

"Here, take these. You'll get a better view," Chris said, handing her a pair of binoculars while positioning himself next to her with his own pair.

Sarah gratefully accepted the binoculars with a big smile and looked through them. "Oh, how neat. I see the nest. Is that the momma osprey on the nest?"

Chris smiled and glanced away from his binoculars to look at Sarah. "Yes, and I bet that male osprey over there, the one that just caught that fish, is going to carry it back to that nest."

"Oh, you're right. Look, he's bringing it back to the nest," Sarah said, awe in her voice.

Chris leaned his arms on the railing and focused his binoculars. "You know, it's the male's job to both protect the nest and bring food to the nest during incubation. The female will also protect the nest along with him, but it's a nice team system they've got going." Chris glanced back at Sarah with a smile.

Sarah's heart skipped a beat and she subtly tried to hide her face since she found herself flushing. How did Chris make the concept of birds nesting sound romantic?

After ten minutes of bird-watching had passed, Chris walked back inside the covered portion of the boat, started up the engine, and took the wheel. "I'm going to bring us around to a little spot I think might have a lot of white egrets and herons for us to watch."

Sarah admired the tranquility of the calm water and gazed at the sun that had just started to set in the distance, feeling happiness overcome her. Boating life sure seemed to suit her. She had only been on a boat a couple of times as a kid for family activities, and never really knew what she was missing, until she met Chris. He opened her eyes and soul to a whole new world she didn't know existed. The serenity and peace that enveloped her on the calm water made her relish every moment. She yearned to be on that boat any chance she had.

Chris ran daily tours on the well-kept, roomy, comfortable boat. His tours mainly took place from April to October, and busy season was just starting to arrive now that it was May.

Sarah walked inside the boat's cabin, sitting at the back while looking out onto the water and watching Chris methodically maneuver the boat. It had only been a little over a month since the couple had started dating, but every minute had been wonderful. Chris had a special aura about him—full of intelligence, wonder, and appreciation of nature. He had a little bit of an unkept, outdated, rustic style to him that made him feel like a man's man, someone who could protect Sarah, just like the male ospreys protect their nests.

When Chris shut the engine down and pulled up to another bird-watching spot, Sarah looked down to see she had a voice mail alert, which was odd since she hadn't heard her phone ring.

She held the phone to her ear to listen, and her stomach dropped. It was Mark, her ex. The one she'd broken up with right before she'd met Chris. They hadn't spoken since and his voice sounded nervous and shaky on the recording.

"Hi, Sarah. It's Mark ... um, I know we're broken up, but I'm home now. I stopped by the coffeehouse today to see you, but they told me you weren't there. I don't know— I guess ... I just wanted to talk. Are you interested in meeting up? Maybe for lunch? I would love to see you."

Sarah dropped her phone back into her purse, knots forming in her stomach.

Chris looked back from the front of the boat, excitement on his handsome face. "There must be hundreds of white egrets over there. See them sitting in the trees?"

Sarah tried to hide her confused face, but it was too late.

"Are you OK? You look like you just saw a ghost," Chris said, more than a little concerned.

Sarah cupped her chin in her hands, took a deep breath, then stood to join Chris. "Yeah, I just received an unexpected voice mail. It took me by surprise."

Chris crinkled his brow, curious about what the voice mail could concern that left Sarah so troubled. Not wanting to pry, he decided against probing further since she clearly didn't feel like talking about it.

Sarah cozied up next to him along the railing and looked out at the beautiful white egrets, then diverted her eyes to the sunset.

Chris followed her gaze momentarily before casting his eyes back on to her. "It's beautiful isn't it? There's something about

3

catching the sunset on the water. I don't know what it is. It's like we have it to ourselves out here."

Sarah smiled, her stomach knots unraveling as her heart lightened again. "Yes, it's amazing and the fact that you get to be on the water for work is something I envy."

She looked over at Chris who'd gone back to watching the egrets. Her heart fluttered as she admired the strong jawbone that peeked out from underneath his beard, the dirty-blond hair poking out from his old fisherman's trucker hat, and the sun freckles on his nose and cheeks. She was attracted to him, there was no denying that, but still—that voice mail stuck in her mind. *Did* she want to talk to Mark? She had broken up with him over the phone, after all, while he'd been away on a long work trip (again). They hadn't seen or talked to each other since.

As the sunset illuminated the sky in hues of pink and orange, the sounds of water softly lapping against the boat's sides and birds calling filled the air. Chris let his binoculars dangle around his neck and gently put his arm around Sarah, who stood close to him by the railing.

"What do you think of all of this? Being out here?" Chris asked, staring intently into Sarah's eyes.

Sarah smiled. "Well, you know I absolutely love being out here. I'm sure you've noticed I can't stop talking about it. Why?"

Chris nodded and looked out towards the sunset that had begun to fade. "I don't know. I guess I just really like having you here with me. I wanted to make sure that you like it too. I really love spending time with you, Sarah. We both do, Sam and I."

Sarah leaned her head on his shoulder. "You're too sweet. Sam is a special little boy. He's lucky to have such a cool, caring, interesting father."

Chris gently rubbed Sarah's back. "Well, his mom is dropping him off at the dock when we get back. He's spending the night at my house. He'll be excited to see you."

Sarah smiled and grabbed his hand as her heart filled to the brim with all of the happiness and love that surrounded her. Chris was exactly what she wanted in a man and he was happy to spend every moment with her, unlike Mark who was never around, so why was she still thinking about Mark since listening to that voice mail? Had everything happened too soon since the break up? Did she need closure? Or was she meant to be with Mark?

* * *

Margaret and Liz perused the bike store for beach cruisers. Margaret wanted to offer bike tours at The Seahorse Inn during the summer, and eyed a seafoam-green bike with high handle bars, a large cushy seat, and a wicker basket and bell. She made a beeline for it, pulling it out to get a feel of it while sitting on it. It was comfy and the handle bars were high enough that her back wouldn't hurt from being hunched over while riding it.

"I love this one. I think this style will be perfect for our guests. We can see if they have them in different colors. I want to get ten for the bike tours," Margaret said as she swiveled the handlebars left and right.

Liz eyed the bike. "It definitely has a retro look that I love. What days are you planning to do the bike tours?"

Margaret paused and thought. "Well, Saturdays and Sundays since those are our busiest days. I figure it will be a three-hour tour with plenty of stops around Cape May for sightseeing and lunch."

Liz smiled. "I love it. It's going to be great. Now remember, we're letting Dolly, Kim, and the new hires take the reins this summer so we can have some much-deserved time off. Don't get too crazy with all of this."

Margaret laughed. "I know. I know. We'll be on that beach every day this summer like you wanted, I promise."

They had come up with a plan of working only a couple of days a week at the inn so they could have the summer (mostly) off. They both had been busy raising families, working normal full-time jobs, and getting the B&B up and running—hustling nonstop—for months now. They were well due for a nice summer break. Plus, Dolly and Kim had proven to be very capable of running the Seahorse over the past few months.

"What going on with Greg's restaurant? Won't you be busy with that all summer, though?"

Liz sighed. "It's supposed to open pretty soon. We're just working out some kinks. But no, I'm letting him handle most of it with his partner. This is his baby. The Seahorse is our baby. I may get more involved eventually."

Just then, a woman walked into the store and immediately started talking to a sales associate until she glanced over at Liz and Margaret.

"Liz? Margaret? How funny to see you here."

Margaret turned to look, then hopped off the bike to give her a hug. "Donna? Oh my goodness! I was wondering when I was going to see you."

Liz smiled. "Long time no see! How have you been, Donna?"

Donna scooped Margaret up for a hug and then Liz. "It's so good to see you two. It feels like forever since I've been back in Cape May ... everything's so weird now with this divorce and all."

Donna was a statuesque five-eleven with shoulder-length straight blonde hair. In high school, she'd starred on the softball team and was one of the most musically gifted students on campus. Her dad was a well-known musician and musical instructor, so he'd taught her just about everything he knew when it came to playing the guitar. Growing up, she constantly wrote music and sang original songs whenever they'd get together. When it came to dating, she could've had just about any guy she wanted, but she'd chosen Adam and they married and moved to California after graduation. Now they were divorcing, and she'd returned home to Cape May to find her roots again.

Margaret put a sympathetic hand on her shoulder. "Well, you know, I've recently been through a divorce myself, so I'm here anytime you need to talk."

Liz nodded her head in agreement. "I'm always around too. Come join Margaret and I on the beach this summer. We plan to be there just about every day—it's a little pact we've made."

Donna's eyes widened. "Are you serious? I would love that. But man, the beaches here don't compare to the ones in California."

Margaret wrinkled her nose, slightly annoyed. "I think you'll remember the magic and unique beauty of Cape May pretty quickly. It's all around you and quite therapeutic. I should know," Margaret said with a wink.

Donna eyed the seafoam-green cruiser Margaret had just been sitting on. "This bike looks exactly like what I came in here to buy. I plan to bike everywhere around town."

Liz laughed. "That's the bike we're about to buy for Margaret's bike tours at the B&B."

Donna smirked. "Well, our good taste surely hasn't changed in years, has it?"

After ordering their bikes and arranging delivery, they ventured out of the store.

A truck horn honked as they made their way to their cars while chatting.

"Dave!" Margaret yelled out.

Dave hung out the window of his truck, smiling from ear to ear. "Hello, ladies. Fancy seeing you out and about. Wait a minute. Donna? Donna Anderson? Is that you?"

Donna laughed. "Oh, it's me, Dave. I'm back in Cape May."

Margaret looked over at Donna, confused. "You know Dave?"

"Yep. My big brother and him were best friends in school. Dave was always hanging around our house," Donna said matter-of-factly.

Dave smiled. "Well, it's great to see you again."

Donna smiled back at Dave, then looked back at Margaret and Liz. "Now how do you two know Dave? I was thinking high school, but he graduated before we even started."

Liz pointed at Margaret and Dave while chuckling "Those two are going steady."

Donna looked back at Dave, who was still smiling ear to ear, but this time staring at Margaret. "Well, that's just too coincidental."

CHAPTER TWO

Memorial Day was three weeks away, and Dave and Margaret, with the help of Margaret's girls, Abby and Harper, were busy planting all of their summer vegetable seeds and seedlings at their garden on Liz and Greg's property.

Margaret admired the beautiful, freshly dug garden plots. "This garden is something. I can't believe we made it twice as big this year. I think I went a little crazy with online seed shopping."

Dave laughed. "Just a little. Your basement looked like a greenhouse with all those seedlings and grow lights. Good thing they're all outside now, hardened off, and ready to plant —otherwise you were about to have a jungle in your home."

Margaret playfully nudged Dave, walked over to the seedling packs and held one up to inspect it. "I have to say, I'm especially excited for all the different varieties of winter squash we're growing this year. The butternut and spaghetti squash grew so prolifically last year, and they kept well all winter. I can't remember how many times I roasted butternut squash for dinner."

Dave rubbed his stomach. "The way you made it with the brown sugar, salt, pepper and olive oil really brought out the sweet and savory. I couldn't get enough. What do you have in your hand there?"

Margaret read the handmade popsicle-stick label in her seedling pot. "Buttercup squash. Supposedly, this squash was bred in the 1920s to taste like a sweet potato. Then down on the ground, I've got sweet dumpling squash, acorn squash, luffa gourds, birdhouse gourds, blue Hubbard squash ... the list goes on."

Abby and Harper ran over, their hands caked with soil. "Mom, we need a few more things to plant in the tea garden," Harper said as they looked through the packs of seedlings.

"Well, how about some chamomile, lemon balm, and apple mint? Those are over there if you want to grab them," Margaret said as she motioned to her left.

They both ran over to grab the seedling packs. Abby stopped to look out towards a small tilled area near the edge of the property by the trees. "That's going to be our own garden, right? Harper and I can plant whatever we want there? It will be the kids' garden?"

Dave looked over at Margaret and smiled. "Yep. That's your area only. We want you two to have your own space to grow whatever you'd like."

Harper squealed. "I can't wait! We're planting over there next. We could grow our own food and bring it up in the tree house to eat, whenever it's finished."

Dave laughed. "Well, I'll get back to work on the tree house for you kids soon. I know you're excited for it. Heck, even I'm excited for a tree house and I'm an adult."

The girls laughed and walked over to plant what they were holding in the tea garden, full of excitement and imagination.

Margaret looked back over at Dave. "So, how's the ol' shore house coming along?"

Dave spun his baseball hat around backwards. "Oh, it's coming. As you know, we closed the deal last week so I'm finally able to get in there and start working. I can't wait to show you this place. How about after we're done here?"

Margaret looked at her watch. "That could work. Maybe bring the girls and try that restaurant near it too?"

Dave smiled. "Sounds perfect."

Margaret thought for a moment. "So … Donna. It's funny that you know her. We grew up together and were friends during school. I'm surprised I never ran into you when I was at her house."

Dave smiled and shrugged. "Guess we always just missed each other. I was good friends with her brother, Joe. I haven't talked to him in years. I wonder what he's up to."

"Did you ever meet Adam, her husband? I guess soon-to-be ex-husband?"

Dave scrunched his brow. "You know, I think I remember meeting him once or twice. He seemed like an OK guy. She did have a huge crush on me for years before she met him, though."

Margaret gave a nervous laugh. "What? That's funny. How did you know that?"

Dave patted the dirt down around a seedling. "Well, let's just say she was being bullied by a kid down the street. I stepped in and stopped it, and then she completely changed around me. Anytime I hung out with Joe, she was there. It became pretty obvious."

Margaret evened out the soil before plunking in some seeds. "So, did anything come of it?"

Dave hesitated. "Not really. Jeez, I can't believe that was over thirty years ago. Crazy how time flies. Can you hand me those tomato packs by you?"

Margaret wanted to know more. What exactly did *not really* mean? He obviously was trying to change the subject.

After a couple more hours of planting in the garden, they called it a day, got their things together, and walked back towards Dave's truck.

"Everyone ready to grab dinner and see my shore house?" Dave asked excitedly.

Harper and Abby jumped up and down.

"I think that's a yes, Dave," Margaret smiled.

They made their way across town to North Cape May and pulled up to a house that faced the Delaware Bay, with just a street between the sand and the house.

"Wow—this is it? This adorable Cape Cod? I guess I could have looked at photos online, but truthfully, I wanted to be surprised," Margaret said.

"This is it, alright. Let's go take a look inside," Dave said as pulled the keys out of the ignition.

The front of the house had an old paint-chipped screened-in porch with Astroturf on the floor. It faced the water, though, so it had that going for it.

Dave put the key into the front door, pushed a couple times, then kicked a few more times before it finally gave way. "I'm going to have to fix that."

The girls and Margaret followed Dave inside the older home.

"Watch out for those nails sticking out of the floorboards there," Dave said motioning to the living room floor.

The girls walked around the house, seemingly bored already and hungry. Meanwhile, Margaret walked towards the bathroom.

"Can I use the bathroom?" Margaret asked.

"Yeah, sure. Go ahead."

Margaret opened the bathroom door into a pink wonderland. Pink tile from floor to ceiling, a pink tub, and a pink toilet. I'm starting to see why he got such a good deal, Margaret thought to herself. *Nothing* had been updated.

Margaret met Dave in the kitchen where he was opening an old window full of cobwebs and dust inside of it. The kitchen had an '80s brown sink, broken and cracked green tiles all over the floor, rotted Formica countertops, and rooster wallpaper. It was just as outdated as the rest of the house. Not to mention, the entire house had an all-around funny smell to it.

"Well, what do you think?" Dave asked optimistically.

Margaret smiled. "The location is great. That's for sure."

Dave opened the oven to find what looked like an animal's nest inside. "Oh, no. It appears animals have been living inside of here."

Abby and Harper, overhearing Dave, squealed. "What kind of animals?"

Dave slammed the oven shut. "Not sure exactly. I'll have to figure out how they're getting inside."

"What about the backyard? Can we look out there?" Margaret asked, trying to find some kind of silver lining.

"Oh yeah, sure," Dave said leading them out the back door.

They walked down crumbling concrete steps to a yard full of rocks and a dilapidated gazebo in the corner.

"My buddy didn't feel like driving here every week to cut the lawn and maintain the yard, so he put all these rocks in," Dave said eyeing the yard.

Margaret and the girls nodded, not thoroughly impressed at all. "Oh, OK."

"Are you all ready to eat? We can walk over to Sunsets at Barry's down the street for dinner. I bet we can get a front-row sunset seat for dinner."

Abby and Harper started walking back inside, ready to leave. "We're starving."

As Margaret followed Dave inside, she shut the back door with its torn screen behind her. "So, what kind of work are you thinking about doing on this place?"

Dave winked. "A lot of work. I didn't want to say anything about that at first. I was kind of seeing how you would react. I have to say, you were very polite about this tattered old place." Dave laughed.

Margaret nudged him. "Let's go get dinner. I'm excited to

try Barry's. I guess we don't get over to North Cape May enough, we've never eaten there."

Dave wrapped his arms around Margaret. "It'll be my first time too. Let's cross our fingers it's good because it's the only place in walking distance."

As they approached the open-air restaurant situated on the corner, they saw the perfect spot to sit, and the hostess happily greeted them before escorting them to their requested table near a fire pit and some cornhole boards. The girls immediately began playing a game as Dave and Margaret ordered food.

The girls giggled while throwing the beanbags at wooden boards with carved-out holes, though they were thoroughly unsuccessful. As the sun slipped over the Delaware Bay across the street, the sky filled with hues of orange and red.

"Here are your fried pickles, chicken fingers, and pizza pie," a young server said as he fumbled with the platters, barely getting them on the table.

Margaret smiled at him then called the girls to come eat, and as a little family, they enjoyed the sunset, food, and ambiance of the quaint corner restaurant.

* * *

Greg walked around the finished restaurant, headed to his favorite area—the basement. After consulting with a few different contractors, he found someone who could transform the basement into a wine cellar seating area. Dark wood floors were installed and stonework had been exposed on the walls. Throughout the wine cellar, wine barrels were strategically placed, rustic light fixtures cast a romantic glow, and wood beams along the ceiling contributed to the organic feel of the perfectly positioned tables and chairs, along with a couple of fancy couches for lounging, in the well-appointed space.

While Greg sat to do paperwork with Italian music blasting

from the new ceiling speakers, back upstairs, the newly hired chef, Ron, worked closely with the line cooks. Opening day was fast approaching and that meant they had to nail down a menu.

Ron, a highly coveted chef who'd worked with many successful restaurants in the Philadelphia and New Jersey area, could take a bland menu and reconstruct it into one of the finest. He was well-known for his culinary talent and to get him on board with Greg's restaurant had been nothing short of a miracle.

Ron rolled his eyes at Ed across from him. "What are you doing? Never *ever* add cumin to my dishes. Do you hear me? I don't know why I have to keep telling you this. No. Cumin. Got it? And you, over there! What's your name?" Ron yelled to one of the cooks in the back.

"Um, Jack," the line cook said even though they had been working together for a couple weeks cooking different dishes and getting the kitchen ready.

"Well, Jack, you're using way too much oil in that pan. Not to mention, the *wrong* oil. No wonder the pan is up in smoke. Have you even cooked before?"

Jack turned red out of both embarrassment and frustration. "Yeah, over at Mammy's Diner for five years."

Ron let out a loud condescending laugh. *"Mammy's Diner?* Are you kidding? That's not cooking. That's … I don't know what that is, but it's nothing like what we're cooking here."

Jack sighed, dumped and cleaned his pan, then started over.

Suddenly, a loud, obnoxious ringtone erupted from Ron's phone, and he walked into the other room to answer it.

Mike, the third line cook, looked over at Jack from his workstation. "Dude, don't take it to heart. He's a bit nuts, I'll admit that, but he knows what he's doing. I worked with him years ago. Not many people last with him, for obvious reasons."

From the other room, Ron snapped at whoever he was speaking on the phone with. "I was told we would get five pounds of fresh blue claw crabs *today*. Not tomorrow. Not in three days. *Today*. Where are they?"

Ron paused as he waited for an answer from the person on the other line. The room and kitchen grew quiet.

Just then everyone jumped as Ron bellowed into his phone. "I don't care if you have to drive them here from Wilmington yourself, you will get them here today. Do I make myself clear?"

After a moment of silence, Ron exploded again, this time taking the call outside where his screaming could most likely be heard down the street.

Ed rolled his eyes as he looked over at Jack and Mike. "Just who does this guy think he is? I'm sorry, but I've worked in plenty of high-end restaurants from here to Philly and I've never encountered such a self-absorbed egotistical tyrant of a chef."

Mike plated the fried artichoke and look over at Ed. "Trust me, I've seen my fair share of cooks walk out on him. I'm not a huge fan of him myself, but I will tell you this, you'll learn."

Jack sighed and plopped some cherry tomatoes into his sizzling pan, then looked at Mike. "Did Ron hire you or something? You sure seem to be taking this in stride. I feel like I'm in a nightmare I can't wake up from."

Mike nodded. "Yeah, he knew I was looking for work, and since he's worked with me before, he likes having me around to count on—but he still yells at me, as you can tell."

Ed chimed in. "And you just put up with that? It's like being bullied around the clock?"

Mike shrugged his shoulder. "Eh, you get used to it. It's not that bad."

Ed and Jack looked at each other and rolled their eyes, not feeling any better about the situation.

Just then, Ron came barreling back inside, phone still in

hand. "Well, I tried, but those blue claws aren't getting here today like they were supposed to. I paid extra to have them here today. I needed us to work on these crab dishes *today*. Suffice it to say, I will probably never use that company again. You only get one strike with Chef Ron."

Jack and Mike swallowed hard as Ron walked over to Mike's artichoke dish, grabbed a fork, and took a bite.

The room became silent once again.

"Good job," Ron said, patting Mike on the back.

Mike exhaled subtly, an internal sigh of relief coursing through him, and smiled. It was one thing to please a chef, and it was another to please Chef Ron.

Ron looked over at Ed's and Jack's greasy mess and winced. He grabbed a fork and spiraled the pasta dish Jack had been working on onto it, then took a bite.

Jack watched, his stomach tied in knots.

"You can't be serious," Ron said tossing his fork across the room, barely making it into the sink. "Your pasta is swimming in oil, it's not al dente, and there is entirely too much salt and not enough flavor in this dish."

Ed cleared his throat.

"I'm not even going to try yours. I've had enough," Ron said to Ed while taking off his chef's jacket.

Ed dumped it in the trash, feeling defeated.

"Clean up and get out of here. I've had enough for today. The blue claws aren't coming, I've got two cooks who need to be taught from scratch, and one who thinks he knows everything, but doesn't. I don't know what I'm going to do with this place," Ron bellowed as he made his way out, slamming the screen door behind him.

Greg, hearing the door slam, made his way upstairs towards the kitchen. "Hey, guys. How's it going? Where's Ron?"

Looking miserable, the three of them sighed as they cleaned up the kitchen. "He left."

Greg furrowed his brow. "He didn't even say goodbye to me. That's odd."

Mike laughed. "No, it really isn't. That's how he is."

Greg shrugged. "Do you guys need help? I'm sure you're about ready to get home at this point."

Jack smiled for probably the first time that day. "No, it's OK, Greg. It won't take too long. Thank you, though."

CHAPTER THREE

Judy and Bob, a little antsy since returning from their long trip in Italy in March, had delved into their hobbies. Judy had gotten more serious about scrapbooking and Bob had taken up fishing.

"Hi, Debbie. I'm about ready to leave. It's the Gray Rabbit Inn, correct?" Judy asked while on the phone.

"That's correct. My friend Ruth runs the place. Linda and Carol will already be there, as well some other ladies. Did you remember we're each bringing one dish to share for the potluck tomorrow night?"

Judy looked at her casserole on the table. "Yep. I made my famous hamburger casserole. I figure it should heat up nicely tomorrow. My GPS says it'll take me about three hours to get there, so I'll see you in a few hours. I can't wait for this scrapbooking weekend—I haven't been to Harrisburg in ages. I'm going to enjoy being with my sisters."

Debbie smiled. "Oh, you're going to love it. The other ladies are fabulous, I think you'll really enjoy yourself. Not sure why you've never joined us in the past. We've been getting together for fifteen years."

Judy looked out at Bob through the window as he was

sorting out his new fishing poles and tackle box in the garage. "Yeah, I guess I'd gotten so used to doing everything with Bob for so many years …. Then, he picked up this new hobby of fishing, and I decided it was time for me to find my own thing too. Welp, I'd better get my things together and go say goodbye to Bob. I'll see you soon."

Judy hung up the phone, zipped up her suitcase, put the cover on her still-warm casserole dish, and made her way to Bob at the garage.

"Hi, hon. Give me a kiss. I'm about ready to head out," Judy said as she leaned in towards him.

Bob gave her a hug and a kiss and grabbed her suitcase. "Are you sure you're OK driving three hours alone?"

Judy followed him to the car as Bob put the suitcase in the trunk. "Oh, I'll be just fine. What I'm worried about is *you*. Will you manage with me gone?" Judy said with a chuckle.

Bob laughed. "Well, dear, this is the first time in thirty years I think we've ever been apart from each other this long. We shall see how I manage. I think there's a couple TV dinners just waiting for me."

Judy rolled her eyes. "I knew I should have made some food for you to warm up while I was gone. Don't eat that junk, it's not good for your high blood pressure and cholesterol."

Bob sheepishly smiled and shut the car door when Judy started the engine.

Judy rolled the window down. "What are your fishing plans?"

Bob glanced at his poles leaning on the garage. "Well, believe it or not, Dan just invited me to go surf fishing with him at Corson's Inlet in Ocean City. He has a permit to drive his truck onto the beach, which is perfect so we don't have to lug all the fishing gear out there. I'm actually quite looking forward to it."

Judy smiled. "That sounds lovely, tell your brother I said

hello. I think I'd like to join you fishing someday. I could bring my chair, beach hat, book, and go look for shells."

Bob daydreamed as he looked off into the distance "That does sound nice. Me fishing and you shelling, then get home in time for a hearty, warm meal and watch our favorite shows. Ah, the retired life. It suits us. Now, you go on and enjoy your weekend in Pennsylvania."

* * *

Sarah crouched on the dock, petting Brewster, the black-and-white dock cat. "Brewster, what do you do all day here besides sleep in the tackle shop? Ever catch any fish?"

Brewster meowed and rubbed against her arm, asking for more pets.

Sarah adjusted her bathing suit straps and stood up as Chris walked over from the boat.

"Well, I think we're all set to head out if you're ready. I see Brewster has found the pretty ladies again. I'm going to put him in the shop before we leave. I don't like him roaming around when I'm not here. I worry too much," Chris said as he gently picked Brewster up in his arms and placed him inside the shop, shutting and locking the door behind him.

Sarah smiled. "So, I made us some sandwiches and snacks for today. I'm pretty excited to meet your friends."

Chris laughed. "I can't wait for you to meet them. Just know they can be a rowdy bunch sometimes. I've got the boat ready and Sam's hanging out in the back of it playing video games. Let's hop on and get going."

Sarah carefully stepped onto the boat and stood at the front, which was the perfect spot for warm sun rays, cool breeze, and sightseeing.

Chris maneuvered the boat out of the dock, steering towards the spot in the bay where his friends would be.

"There they are, those knuckleheads," Chris jokingly said,

fifteen minutes later. He pulled the boat alongside the others in a calm, secluded spot away from everything else.

Jim, Chris's friend, helped Chris get his boat parallel to his. "Bring 'er right on over. You've got it. Move to the left a little more," Jim guided before taking ahold of Chris's boat.

Five boats, all aligned next to each other, made for quite the boat party where you could walk from one boat to the next. Music played, food and drinks lined different areas of each boat, kids played in inner tubes in the water while other folks sunbathed on towels, or just socialized.

Sarah's eyes widened in awe. "How cool is this? So, this what you boat owners do for fun."

Chris put his arms around Sarah. "Well, some of us boat owners anyway. This has been a tradition of ours since growing up together."

Sam finally put his phone down, pulled his shirt off, and threw it on the ground. "Dad, can I go swimming with everyone?"

Chris lowered his sunglasses. "Sure thing. Are you ever going to say hi to Sarah, though? You've been staring at that phone of yours this whole time. I told your mother I didn't want to get you a phone and this is exactly why."

Sam gave a little smirk. "Hi, Sarah. Why don't you come swimming with us?"

Sarah smiled and rustled his hair. "I will eventually. You go out there and enjoy yourself."

Sam made a beeline for the ladder before yelling over to the other kids, who all seemed happy to see him.

"Here, let's walk to the other boats so I can introduce you to everyone," Chris said, taking Sarah's hand to lead her onto the next boat.

"You must be Jim," Sarah said while extending her hand.

Jim pulled her in for a bear hug. "We don't do handshakes in these parts. It's all hugs here. By the way, this is my wife,

Melissa, and our kids, Joshua and Jackson are in the water. We've heard a lot about you from Chris."

Melissa waved from her sunbathing spot. "So nice to meet you, Sarah."

After making the rounds to the other boats and meeting everyone else, Sarah was chitchatting with Melissa when Chris's cell phone rang and he walked to the back of the boat to take the call.

"Yes, I'll have him home by five … Don't worry … No, he hasn't had any candy. Yes, I have been keeping an eye on him. We all have been watching the kids."

Sarah looked over at Melissa, confused by the phone call. "It's his ex-wife, Roberta. Sam's mom. She's been like this ever since the divorce. She literally calls him like ten times a day," Melissa said as she glanced over at Chris on the phone.

Sarah, not knowing what to say, felt uncomfortable with the whole situation. "Interesting."

Melissa looked back over at Sarah. "You know, he hasn't dated anyone since her, and they got divorced five years ago. Honestly, we thought she was ruining any chance he would have with someone else."

Sarah gulped hard. "Oh, really?"

"Yeah. I'm not trying to scare you away, though. We love Chris and want to see him with someone good for him for once. He's been through a lot. I guess I may have said too much," Melissa said as she watched her kids play in the water.

Sarah thought for a moment. "Oh, no. It's fine. It's good to know these things. I'm just surprised I've never heard her call him before. We've been spending so much time together lately."

Melissa scrunched her brow. "Yeah, I'm surprised too. We're all used to it around here. Roberta never took to us, never had any interest in hanging out, which caused Chris to be around less. We're all so glad they divorced."

Sarah, a little overwhelmed with all of the information, took a deep breath and exhaled.

"I'm going to go in the water to cool off," Sarah said as she pulled her shirt off to reveal her bathing suit, and headed to the ladder before glancing over at Chris who was still pacing with the phone to his ear.

"Here's a float, Sarah," Sam said, happy to see she was joining them in the water.

Sarah gratefully grabbed the lounge-chair float, hoisted herself on, and laid back, luxuriating in the sun and splashing some water on herself. The water was very cold, as it was only May after all, but the temperature was already in the eighties, which made a dip in the water nice.

Just then, a loud splash and a big wave tossed Sara's float around and soaked her bathing suit through as Chris dove into the water from the boat. Popping his head up from the water, he threw a foam football to the kids, and then fixed his eyes on Sarah. "Hey, you."

"Hey, there," Sarah said, not sure whether it was appropriate to bring up his phone call. They had only been dating for a month and a half, was it her place to ask?

Chris playfully splashed her. "Come in the water. It's nice."

Sarah chuckled, adjusted her sunglasses, and spread out in an exaggerated way on the float. "I am in the water, silly. I'm on a float *in the water*. See?"

Chris smirked, and sneakily swam up behind her lounge chair's back, overturning it into the water in slow motion.

"Ahhhh! What are you doing? I'm so comfortable," Sarah yelled, fruitlessly clinging to the float for dear life as she toppled over into the cold water.

When she surfaced, she slicked her hair back, sporting a look of annoyance. "Really? Did you *really* do that?"

Chris shrugged and laughed good-naturedly. "Well, it got you in, which is where I wanted you to be."

Sarah sighed and smiled. "Here I am. Now what?"

Chris swam closer to Sarah, wanting to touch and pull her close to hold her. Instead, he grabbed her hand under the water.

"Are you having fun?" he asked, blocking the football that hurtled straight for Sarah's head all the while still holding her hand underwater.

Sarah smiled, a warm feeling shooting through her body in the freezing water. "Yes, I am. You were on your phone, I saw?"

Dave threw the football back to the kids, then ran his fingers through his wet hair. "Yeah, about that—"

Just then, Jim and the other guys cannonballed into the water beside Sarah and Chris causing waves and splashing and totally interrupting the conversation Sarah had worked up the nerve to start.

* * *

Meanwhile across town, Donna was settling in—though life felt very unsettled, generally speaking—at her parents' house. She had to keep telling herself it was a temporary situation; she'd only be there until she got back on her feet again.

Donna dramatically flopped down onto the twin bed still residing in her old bedroom. Her parents hadn't changed much in the room, aside from adding a sewing area for her mother, since she moved out during college over twenty-seven years ago. She looked up at the unicorn paper trim lining the top of the wall around the room. On the nightstand stood an '80s alarm clock with a framed signed photo of New Kids on the Block from when she'd seen them in concert when she was fourteen. In the corner sat a rocking chair piled high with her old stuffed animals. Above, on a shelf, the many softball trophies she'd received throughout grade school stood in a line.

"This is literally history preserved. This room is frozen in time," Donna said out loud to nobody as she got up to go look in the closet.

After sliding the door open, a small chest with a lock on it sat in plain view on the top shelf.

"You're kidding. I haven't opened this since I was eighteen," Donna said aloud, pulling it down to the ground and fiddling with the chest lock.

Just then, her mother knocked on the door. "Are you making out OK, dear?"

Donna, growing frustrated with the lock and starting to search for the key, stopped and took a deep breath. "I think so. Thanks, Mom. You can open the door if you'd like."

Janet opened the door, her short tight curls laid perfectly around her head in the same hairstyle she'd worn Donna's entire life. They weren't much for change, Donna's parents. "I brought you some towels and washcloths for the shower. Do you need anything else?"

"Oh, that's perfect. Thank you, Mom. Say, do you know where the key is to the lock for my old chest? I haven't opened that thing in twenty-seven years. I'm dying to see what's inside," Donna said as she searched the dresser drawers.

Janet laughed. "Oh, that ole thing. We always wondered what was in there that was so important to be locked up. We haven't a clue. Never saw it around anywhere."

Donna sighed and grabbed a dusty pink radio from one of the drawers and plugged it in. "Now this has to be an antique."

She turned the radio to a station playing older music and sat on the floor, leaning against the bed. "I mean, I know I've been back here many times since I left for college, but I never went through my old stuff. No idea why. I guess my split from Adam, the soon-to-be divorce, and living here again is really hitting home. Maybe I'll find comfort in nostalgia more so now than ever."

Janet nodded, walked over, and put her hand on Donna's shoulder. "Well, your father and I will always be here for you.

We know you're going through a tough time, but we do love having you home. Your father would love to play guitar with you again, like the old days."

Donna sighed and put her hand on top of her mom's. "To be honest, I haven't played guitar in years. It just got away from me in California. Our life was so busy. I do love being back here, but I really miss California. I miss my life there. Sometimes, I even miss Adam. I miss my job. I don't know what's going on with me. I guess I'm here to figure it all out."

Janet picked up a Strawberry Shortcake figurine that had fallen beside the sewing table. "I think you need to get out. See your friends. Maybe get to *really* know Cape May again."

Donna nodded. "You're right. I guess my hometown always had this stigma to me growing up. I couldn't wait to leave and see the world. Moving back felt like a step in the opposite direction."

Janet scoffed. "I'll have you know that Cape May is listed as one of the top beach towns in the country in a magazine I read. How many beach towns do you know with tons of historic beautiful Victorian houses, horse carriages, wineries, breweries, adorable shops and eateries—"

Donna cut in. "OK, I get it. I need to see my hometown as an enlightened open-minded adult and not a jaded teenager. Now to just figure out how to open this chest. I can't remember what's in it, but somehow I feel like it might be important."

CHAPTER FOUR

The next morning, after settling in the night prior, Judy met the ladies in the dining room for breakfast. Gray Rabbit Inn was a cozy little bed and breakfast with a huge room next to the kitchen perfect for a gal's scrapbooking getaway.

Judy sat down next to Linda at the table. "What's for breakfast this morning?"

Before Linda could answer, the inn owner, Sherry, walked right over holding two pitchers. "Would you care for fresh-squeezed orange juice or some hot coffee?"

"Oh, how lovely. I'll take one of each," Judy said with a chuckle.

Sherry poured the drinks for Judy while Debbie and Carol, having slept in a little longer, came over to join them.

"I hear breakfast is a sweet potato hash with eggs and their famous stuffed French toast," Linda said to the group.

"That sounds lovely. What's the French toast stuffed with?" Debbie asked as she put her napkin in her lap.

Sherry, having overheard the conversation, placed the breakfast plates in front of them. "A sweetened cream cheese. It's delicious."

The ladies looked at each other with eyes widened in

excitement as they grabbed their forks and knives and started in on the most delicious breakfast any of them had seen in a while.

Judy sipped her coffee, took a deep breath, and savored this time with her sisters. "What's the itinerary for the rest of the day? I know you all have been doing this for years. I feel like a newbie."

Carol pulled her written itinerary from her purse and placed it on the table. "Well, after breakfast, we head to that big room over there," she gestured over her shoulder, "set up our scrapbooking stations, put some music on, and get to work. I'm finishing my scrapbook for Michelle's fortieth birthday. It has all of her photos and memories from growing up. I'm going to surprise her with it on the big day. What are you working on?"

Judy took her last bite of French toast and washed it down with orange juice. "Well, I thought about doing one for our recent trip to Italy. That trip has been on my mind a lot lately. Not only did we make so many memories, but it strengthened our marriage, especially right at a time when things were starting to feel monotonous."

Carol nodded in agreement. "That's wonderful. Any other trips in the future planned?"

Judy smiled. "Well, nothing yet, but I'm pretty excited to tag along with Bob on his fishing excursions this summer, which reminds me. I need to call him to see how it's going over at Corson's Inlet today. He's surf fishing with his brother Dan. I'll be right back."

Judy grabbed her phone, excused herself from the table and walked back up to her bedroom.

Sherry and another inn worker came by. "Is everyone finished up here? We can start taking plates." When ladies at the table moaned from their full bellies and pushed their plates away from them, Sherry said, "I'll take that as a yes," with a chuckle.

Ruth, the organizer of the weekend, stood up at the end of the table. "Now that you've had your breakfast and coffee, I thought I'd introduce myself to the new folks. I'm Ruth. I've been putting together this scrapbooking weekend for fifteen years now. We are going to go to the sunroom and start getting to work on our scrapbooking now. I hope you're all ready to make new memories while putting together your scrapbook!"

The group stood from the table, and though they were full, they were also excited to have a day full of reminiscing, creativity, and conversation.

Upstairs, Judy dialed Bob's cell phone, and he answered out of breath, with shouts and loud sounds behind him. "Hello, dear. How is everything?"

"We just finished breakfast and are about to start scrapbooking. I figured now was a good time to call and check in to make sure everything is alright," Judy said, a little confused by the background noise.

Bob paused and yelled over to someone. "It's just sinking in the sand! It's not working! Sorry, hon. My brother's truck is stuck in the sand on the beach. We just finished up an early morning of surf fishing and the tide crept up on us. We lost track of time."

"What? Are you serious? Can you get it out?" Judy asked, surprised.

Bob yelled again, "Put it in reverse! You're now in a hole!" to his brother before addressing his wife. "Sorry about that. I sure hope we can get it out. The tide came in way too quickly, and if we don't get this truck out soon, it'll be swallowed up by the ocean."

"Oh no! Can't anyone there help you?" Judy asked, growing concerned.

Bob sighed. "Welp, unfortunately the only other trucks that were here have already left, so we're stuck."

Judy thought for a moment. "Dave has a truck. How about

I call Margaret and see if he's available? Cape May is a good forty minutes away, though. Do you have enough time?"

"I think it will come down to the wire, but it may just work. Let me go talk to my brother. I will call back in a bit," Bob said, sounding overwhelmed.

Judy immediately dialed Margaret after Bob disconnected.

Margaret answered by the third ring. "Hey Mom. What's up?"

"Margaret, we need your help. Are you with Dave? Dad is with Uncle Dan in Ocean City at Corson's Inlet, and your uncle's truck is stuck in the sand with the tide coming in. They need help. Probably another truck to pull them out immediately."

Margaret relayed to Dave, who had paused working on his beach house, telling him what was going on.

"OK, Mom. We're leaving now. Let Dad know," Margaret said as she hung up the phone.

By the time Margaret got outside, Dave was talking to Chris, and it was the first time she'd seen him at his house since she'd heard he lived next door.

"Do you want me to take you guys in my truck? It might be able to handle this situation better. I'm used to towing boats, and it's got some great horse power," Chris said after Dave had quickly filled him in.

Dave nodded. "Yep, my truck is on the older side. That'd be awesome if you could do that. We really have to hurry as the tide is coming in, if that's alright."

Chris pulled the keys out of his pocket, popped his sunglasses on, and hopped in the truck. "Get in. We've got no time to waste. My buddy had the same thing happen years ago, and it wasn't a pretty situation."

Dave and Margaret hopped in as Chris hit the road towards Corson's Inlet.

"Welp, I hope we can get them out. May have to put the

pedal to the metal here to make good time. They know we're coming?" Chris asked.

"Yep," Margaret said from the back seat.

Conversation ceased in the truck for a bit as the windows were down and the loud wind whipped against their hair and ears.

"So, it's nice to finally meet you, Chris. I'm Margaret," she practically shouted over the wind.

Chris rolled the windows up partially to be able to hear better. "Yes, it's great to meet you. Dave's got a nice a fixer-upper over there. It's nice to see someone is going to clean that place up."

Dave nodded. "Yep. I can't wait, and hey, I've got some cool neighbors to boot."

Margaret bit her lip. "Do you know who I am, Chris?"

Chris looked in his rearview mirror at Margaret. "You're Dave's girlfriend, right?"

"Well, yes, but I'm also Sarah's good friend," Margaret said.

Chris lowered his sunglasses and again looked in the rearview mirror while driving. "You're kidding. You're friends with Sarah?"

Margaret rolled her eyes and playfully nudged Dave. "Yeah, I'm guessing Dave never got around to telling you that. She's one of my best friends."

Chris smiled and blushed, feeling happier at the sound of Sarah's name. "Well, that is just too funny. Did you not tell Sarah about Dave moving next door to me?"

Margaret turned to glance out the back window. "You know, it's funny. I was waiting until Dave closed on the house first before I told more people. I didn't want to jinx anything."

Chris threw his arm over the seat. "Yes, nice to meet you too. Sarah is a pretty extraordinary person."

Margaret smiled on the inside, happy that someone special

was in Sarah's life again, and actually had time to spend with her, unlike Mark.

Thirty-five minutes later, they arrived to Corson's Inlet. Chris had a permit of his own and knew the area well, which helped them get to Bob and Dan faster. Chris pulled the truck around so it backed right up to the front of Dan's truck.

Dave and Chris swiftly hopped out of the truck, ready to get down to business, while Margaret followed behind.

Bob stared at the tide creeping closer and closer. "Thank you, guys, for coming to bail us out. We're down to minutes here. I really hope this works."

Dan shook his head as he kept trying to dig sand away from the wheels.

"I've got a tow strap. We'll hook your truck to mine and pull you out. How does that sound?" Chris asked as he grabbed the strap.

Dan, feeling exhausted, threw the shovel down and climbed in the driver's side of the truck, ready to accelerate. "Sounds perfect. I don't think an old guy like myself can keep digging to China."

Dave grabbed the strap from Chris and quickly secured the trucks together while Chris hopped back in the truck and started the engine. "OK, the straps are secure. Hit the gas," Dave said, keeping an eye on everything.

Chris and Dan both accelerated their trucks, but Dan's wheels kept spinning in the sand, while the ocean tide was a mere foot away from the wheels.

Chris yelled from the truck. "Dave and Margaret, do you see any cardboard in the back of my truck?"

Margaret ran over to look. "Yes, there are a few boxes."

"Perfect. Let's open them up and put them in front of Dan's wheels to provide better traction." Chris quickly hopped back out of the truck.

Bob ran over to help open the cardboard boxes and lay them in front of the truck's wheels. It was truly a team effort.

However, the tide had come up under Dan's truck and on the wheels.

Dave gave the thumbs up to Chris and Dan. "All good. Let's give it a go. We've got to get this truck out *now!*"

Chris and Dan each pushed their gas pedals hard, and the boxes provided enough traction under Dan's tires that the truck moved all the way out of the sand pit it was in.

Everyone high fived, said their thank yous, and ran back to their trucks to quickly head out of there before the tide got any higher.

"Thank you so much, Chris and Dave. I don't know what I would have done without you two to help with my dad and uncle," Margaret said as she hopped in the back seat behind Dave.

Dave reached his hand behind his seat and gently squeezed Margaret's, making her feel relieved, calm, and loved.

"No problem. I'm happy to help," Chris said as he steered his truck off the beach.

Dave thought for a moment as he stared out the window. "Why don't we all get together and hang out sometime? A couples kinda thing."

Margaret laughed. "You read my mind, Dave. I need to talk to Sarah. Does that sound good, Chris?"

Chris's phone suddenly rang. He quickly glanced at it and shook his head, letting it go to voice mail. "Sounds perfect."

* * *

Back at the restaurant, Greg still had to come up with a name and nail down a menu. He had just gotten situated at a table with his papers and laptop when Chef Ron announced he and the cooks were finishing up final touches on some different plates.

"Hey, Greg. We've got some dishes for you to try. I think they'd be great for the menu," Ron said from the kitchen.

"Perfect," Greg said, rubbing his hands together in anticipation.

Ron walked over with the first couple of dishes and placed them on the table. "I was thinking a new-age Italian style would complement this restaurant nicely."

"Oh. I thought we decided on rustic Italian comfort food?" Greg asked, confused.

"Well, just try these first. This here is what I call an Italian sushi. Instead of seaweed, it's prosciutto, and instead of raw fish, it's roasted zucchini and fresh arugula with lemon drizzle," Ron said as he motioned for Greg to taste it.

Greg took a bite. "Well, it's good … but …"

Ron cut him off before he could get out another word. "Now try this one. It's polenta with peas, anchovies, and a strawberry drizzle."

Greg nearly gagged at the description, before hesitantly taking a bite to appease Ron. "It's, um, interesting."

Ron was shocked. "What? You don't like it? How can you not?"

Greg swallowed hard and wiped his mouth. "Ron, this is very innovative, but I don't think it's the Italian style we discussed; it's not what I wanted for my restaurant. I wouldn't mind some interesting outside-of-the-box dishes, but *not* this interesting. Plus, I want to keep it as rustic as possible, like going-to-your-nonna's-house-for-Sunday-gravy kind of style. A place where customers feel at home because everything is wonderful and familiar."

Ron stood up, threw his towel on the ground, and aggressively grabbed the plates on the table. "Fine, whatever. Do what you want. If you want boring eggplant parmigiana and over-done spaghetti and meatballs, be my guest."

Greg, realizing that he'd offended Ron, sighed. "Ron. I just don't think these types of dishes will sell to the crowd that I'm marketing to. I have to keep in mind what the people are going to want. I'm not going to make any profits otherwise."

Ron scoffed, walked in the kitchen, dropped the dishes into the sink, which caused a loud clatter. "Clean those up when you get a second, guys. We have to start from scratch," Ron said to Ed, Jack, and Mike.

Greg approached Ron to try and make peace. He wasn't looking to aggravate his chef, especially when the excitement of opening the restaurant filled the air. "Look, I'm sorry. I liked your dishes, but we need to meet in the middle somewhere."

Ron walked over to his chef knives, put them away, and pulled off his chef jacket. "Whatever. I need to leave. Maybe you can come up with some kind of menu on your own."

"What? No. Why are you saying that?" Greg asked, growing concerned.

Mike, Ed, and Jack, while washing and drying the dirty dishes and utensils, paused to listen in. They sure knew how volatile Chef Ron could be, and the scene playing out was like watching a straight-up soap opera.

Ron let out an aggressive sigh and walked towards the front door. "I don't know. I just have things on my mind. I need to leave. Now, excuse me."

Greg watched as Ron left, slamming the door behind him. He let out a loud groan and walked towards the kitchen.

"I'm sorry you guys have to put up with this. I had no idea," Greg said as he leaned on the door frame to the kitchen.

Mike laughed. "Oh, we're used to it, especially me. I've worked with Chef Ron before. I overheard you discussing what kind of Italian style food you were looking for. It's the kind I was trained in and cooked at my previous jobs. I know exactly what you're trying to go for."

Greg sighed. "Thanks, Mike. I'm glad to have someone here understand. You guys can finish up and head home early. I'm just going to get some paperwork done."

CHAPTER FIVE

"Hop on! Let's go!" Margaret yelled over to Dave as she sat on the beach cruiser in front of The Seahorse Inn.

Dave fumbled with an air pump. "Well, this tire is just about full. Where are we off to?"

Margaret, feeling impatient and like she was twelve again, took off on her bike down Beach Avenue before whipping around to Dave. "This bike feels fabulous. I'm like a kid again. They're perfect for the bike tours that will start Memorial Day Weekend. My gosh, it's only a week away. I have an idea of a planned route around Cape May for these tours, and I want us to ride it today."

Dave turned his hat around backwards, and flipped his wayfarer sunglasses down. "OK, I'll follow your lead. I'll pretend I'm a guest at the inn. Surprise me."

Margaret looked up at the sun and smiled, letting the warm, bright rays soothe her skin. She adjusted her baseball cap and wearing her cutoff overalls, set out on her course. She'd had this tour route in her head for a month and was finally able to bike it this morning.

Margaret watched the ocean on one side and looked at the beautiful Victorian houses on the other until eventually riding up onto the Cape May Promenade, a two-mile paved walkway that ran parallel to Beach Avenue. The promenade had been a wooden boardwalk once upon a time but was demolished in the nor'easter back in 1962.

Margaret and Dave passed the early morning walkers and bikers enjoying the sun and salt water air. Every person they passed politely nodded or waved as they glided by on their cruisers.

Turning down a tree-lined street full of beautiful Victorian bed-and-breakfasts and homes, they passed an old hotel that had a lovely restaurant with an outdoor porch. The restaurant was known for their delicious brunch, and Margaret's mouth watered at the thought of it. It was fun to see everyone outside enjoying their meals.

"What do you think so far?" Margaret asked over her shoulder as Dave happily pedaled along.

Dave rang the bell on his bike a few times, which caused some pedestrians to stop and look. "It's great. I feel like a visitor in my own town."

Margaret laughed, stood up on the bike, and pedaled faster, the beauty of Cape May whizzing by them. When she arrived at Broadway Avenue, she turned and glided by a taco stand and flea market, among other places, before stopping in front of Greg's soon-to-be restaurant, waiting for Dave to catch up.

"You know, you may have to be a little slower for the folks on the tour. Just saying," he teased when he stopped next to her.

Margaret playfully nudged him. "So, I have an idea that involves Greg's restaurant whenever it opens. I talked to him, and he's going to make us a little sitting area off to the side out back where we can try an assortment of appetizers and relax for a little bit. He was pretty excited about it because it'll help spread the word about his new place."

Dave nodded. "I like it. Good thinking."

Margaret hopped back on her bike. "OK, follow me." She

steered towards Sunset Boulevard, then turned down a little side street, before pulling into a long gravel driveway that led to a big farm and market.

"Wow. How have I never known this was here?" Dave said, as he locked his bike up to the fence next to Margaret's.

Margaret's eyes widened and as she made her way through all of the loose chickens walking around, she bent down to touch and smell the fresh herbs growing in raised beds. Lavender, rosemary, chives, and basil—their aromas filled her nose.

"I love it here. My happy place. It reminds me of our garden, but so much more expansive. The market is dreamy. Come on in," Margaret said as she grabbed his hand and led him through the front doors.

Dave walked in and immediately gravitated to the freshly picked floral bouquets and artisan peanut butters, red sauces, and jarred pickled items. He browsed dispensers of freshly made teas full of herbs from the gardens, grabbed a paper cup, and helped himself.

Margaret walked over holding hand-poured rosemary-mint candles. "Smell this. It's so refreshing."

Dave inhaled the soy candle. "Smells nice and clean. Reminds me of an old shampoo I had that made my head tingle."

Margaret walked over to the pickled items, holding up some pickled beets in red wine. "I need these in my life. I need to get out of here before I buy the entire market. I'm thinking this will be a perfect stop for the bike tour. Good thing the bikes have baskets on them."

They bought their items and headed out to the back gardens to meander among the wide variety of vegetable plants and picnic tables with umbrellas for shade.

"Where are those people walking to?" Dave asked, pointing towards the parking lot.

Margaret grabbed his hand. "Oh, there are ducks, pigs,

geese, beehives, and larger garden plots down that dirt road. It's wonderful. You have to see it."

After roaming around the farm and savoring the beauty and life all around them, they hopped back on their bikes.

"OK, time for the next stop. It's right down the road," Margaret said as she placed her items in the basket and took off.

Minutes later, and they arrived at a winery with another long, winding driveway. They passed beautiful vineyards in the front and had to dodge more chickens foraging for food before they breezed towards a grand building with a lovely patio and outdoor seating.

Margaret talked with the host before they were shown to a shady seating area off to the side. "So, why are we here? you may be wondering. Well, the owner is going to have someone give a mini tour-within-a-tour to my participants about the vineyard and winery and how it all works. Then, afterwards we'll enjoy some small snacks and a wine tasting. Nothing crazy since we'll be biking afterwards."

Dave smiled. "Did you order us something? Because that server is walking this way with some plates."

Margaret gave a mischievous grin. "Maybe."

The server placed a creamy mushroom toast and some gorgonzola stuffed olives in front of them while another server deposited water glasses on the table.

"Wow. This looks great," Dave said, eyeing the food.

Margaret stabbed her fork into an olive and popped it into her mouth. "Dive in. Just a little snack for us before we continue on."

After their winery excursion, they were off towards Sunset Boulevard again.

Margaret happily pedaled along, smiling while looking over her shoulder at Dave. "We have another stop."

Dave followed as Margaret steered straight towards Sunset

Beach. When they arrived, they locked their bikes up, took their shoes and socks off, and walked out to the sand.

Margaret thought for a moment, then got a bright idea. "Let's walk that way down the beach."

Dave walked beside her, taking her hand in his, feeling excited for Margaret and her perfectly executed bike tour.

"So, I'm thinking I'll talk to my group about the Cape May Diamonds, the old shipwreck out in the water, and there's one other thing I'd like to show them if it's there," Margaret said, staring down the beach.

About a half mile of walking later, they arrived to a set of train tracks in the sand.

Dave crouched down to run his finger over them. "I've heard about these tracks but always miss seeing them. They only show up a couple of times a year at low tide."

Margaret squatted next to him to inspect the tracks and take photos with her phone. "Yep. It's fascinating, isn't it? It's so crazy to see it unearth itself on this beach. I've read it's from the early 1900s. Of course, I can't guarantee it will be here for every tour, but it's wonderful to see nonetheless."

After taking photos and admiring the historical artifacts, they walked back towards the bikes, making sure to relish the soothing ocean and cool sand along the way.

Just as they got back to their bikes, Dave's voice mail dinged. He looked at it. "Brad? It's my sister's boyfriend—I haven't talked to him since the film ended. Let me see what he wants."

Dave listened to his voice mail. "Hey, Dave, it's Brad. I'm calling because I'm worried about Irene. She went on a hike this morning with the dog, and she's usually back by now. I can't get ahold of her. I know I might be jumping the gun, but I'm kind of freaking out. Give me a call back."

Dave held the phone and looked over at Margaret. "He's worried about my sister. He thinks she's lost on her hike."

Margaret held her hand to her mouth. "Oh, no."

Dave dialed Brad back instantly. It went to voice mail, so he called again. Voice mail picked up again. And then again after that.

Margaret waited with baited breath. "Anything?"

Dave shook his head. "My anxiety just shot through the roof, and I'm three thousand miles away. I feel helpless. I'm not even sure if I should call my parents or siblings. I don't want to worry them. Let's just sit on the beach for a bit until I hear back from him. I won't be able to answer my phone if I'm riding the bike."

After waiting what felt like an eternity sitting at the beach, but was really a half hour, Brad finally called back. Dave put the phone on speaker for Margaret to hear. "I'm sorry to worry you all, she finally got ahold of me. Her cell phone lost reception, and she ended up hiking a different trail that made her a little lost, but she figured it out and is home now. I'm just a nervous boyfriend, I guess," Brad said, sounding relieved.

Dave took a deep breath and exhaled, his stress slowly abating. Meanwhile, he pulled Margaret in as close as possible and looked at her. "It just means you care, Brad. Nothing to be sorry about. It did shake us up a little, but I'm so glad she's home."

Brad gave a nervous chuckle. "Yeah, we both agreed that she needs to find a hiking group or only do hikes she knows well alone. It gave us a both a scare. Here, I'll let her tell you the story."

"Hey, guys," Irene said. "You wouldn't believe it. I ended up on this gorgeous trail with Brady, our dog. I'm following the blazes for the trail when suddenly, I can't figure out where I am, and there were no blazes in sight. I kept walking, thinking I'd figure it out, but the trail just got narrower and the brush thicker. It spiraled from there. I ended up lost, not sure which way I'd come from or was headed to, and covered in ticks. I finally somehow ended up in a woman's backyard, I kid you not. I was walking down the driveway to the street just as she arrived home. She pulled over to see why I was in her yard and after explaining to her that I was lost, she drove me to my car five miles down the road in the parking lot. Not doing that again, that's for sure. But it's definitely something I can laugh about now."

Margaret grabbed Dave's hand. "Well, we are so glad you're home now. You know I have a hiking group here that I love. I'm sure you can find a great one in your area. And that Brad, he's a keeper," Margaret said.

"I know. He is pretty wonderful. I'll let you two get back to whatever you were doing. Thanks for being a caring ear for Brad."

Dave ended the call and looked over at Margaret. "Well, I wasn't expecting this wonderful day to take such a turn."

Margaret sighed and smiled. "Well, if you're up for it, I have one more planned stop."

Dave hopped up and brushed the sand off himself. "I'm definitely up for it."

Back on the bikes, Margaret lead the way to a lobster seafood restaurant on the harbor.

Dave chuckled. "Ah, my favorite restaurant in the area. What's your plan here?"

Margaret smiled and grabbed his hand after they'd locked their bikes up. "It's a surprise that I think both you and my tour participants will love."

Margaret ordered at the front, and they found a little table outside on the deck by the water.

Moments later, the server arrived with two plates of the restaurant's famous bread pudding.

Dave's eyes widened at the wonderful smell of the dessert paired with the decadent caramel drizzle.

Margaret grabbed her fork and took a bite. "This is the grand finale. What do you think?"

Dave took a bite and closed his eyes, listening to the sound of seagulls and boats going by in the harbor. "This is pure bliss,

Margaret. I think you're really highlighting some wonderful places here in Cape May. How could anyone not fall in love with this beach town?"

* * *

Liz stood at her son's soccer game, pacing the sidelines as Steven dribbled the ball towards the net and narrowly missed the goal.

"Oh! You almost had it, Steven. Good effort!" Liz yelled, cupping her hands around her mouth and then clapping.

Further down the line from her, she noticed her son's coach throw his clipboard down in frustration before turning around to fill a cup of water from the dispenser on the bench.

Liz rolled her eyes and muttered to herself, "Well, Coach Will, if he had someone to pass to, that would've helped. He had nowhere to go and the other team's defense was all over him."

Liz felt a tap on her shoulder, and turned around. "Donna! I'm so glad you could make it," Liz said as she pulled her in for a hug.

Donna smiled. "I'm just glad to spend some time with my friend, and of course see Steven play. Where's Michael?"

Liz looked at the time on her phone. "Greg's picking him up from baseball practice and taking him back to the restaurant. Did you want to swing by and see the restaurant with me after the game?"

The ref whistled at a foul, startling both Liz and Donna, since they hadn't been paying much attention to the game.

"Yeah, I'm definitely up for that. How's the restaurant coming along? Is there an opening date yet?" Donna asked.

Liz rolled her eyes. "Oh, yeah ... that part. Well, he's having some issues with the chef he hired. They can't seem to agree on much. So, who knows when he'll officially open. I think he's hoping for a June date, but we'll see."

Meanwhile at the restaurant, Greg was stressed. His chef hadn't arrived like he'd said he would, and after he stormed out yesterday, Greg wasn't even sure if he still had a chef. Thankfully, the cooks were working on different dishes, and so far, they'd proved to be much more friendly and reliable than Ron.

Greg dialed Dale, his friend who owned the successful restaurant Porridge in Collingwood.

"Hey, Greg, my man! What's up? How's it going at the restaurant? I've been meaning to call you. We haven't talked in a month or so, and I said I'd mentor you along the way. It's just been nuts around here lately," Dale said while pots and pans clanged in the background.

"Dale. It's so good to talk to you. Everything was running pretty well until yesterday when my chef stormed out over a disagreement on the menu," Greg said, pacing the restaurant.

Dale sighed. "You're kidding. Who's the chef you hired?"

Greg gulped. "Chef Ron."

Daled paused. "As in Chef Ron Whittaker?"

"Yep."

Dale sighed. "Well, that's your first problem. Ron is notorious for being erratic and uncompromising. Great chef, but I would, personally, never be able to work with a chef like that in my restaurant."

Greg shook his head. "This is terrible. I knew I should have consulted you before I hired him. What do I do now?"

Dale looked at his watch. "Well, I'm actually in Ocean City helping a buddy. How about I meet you at your restaurant in an hour. We'll figure this out."

"You could do that? You don't know what this means to me, Dale. Thank you. I'm going to go pick up my son at practice. I'll see you when you get here," Greg said, feeling more relieved than ever.

An hour later, Dale walked inside and gave Greg a hand-shake and back pat. "This place is wonderful. It has so much character. Can I take a look around?"

Greg felt giddy at the thought of showing Dale around the place. "Oh yes, but wait until you see the wine cellar area in the basement. It's my favorite part."

After a full tour, they made their way back upstairs and Dale introduced himself to the cooks. "What are you guys cooking up?"

Mike happily spoke up. "Well, this is an idea I came up with for Greg's eggplant parm dish. It's done, if you want to try it."

Dale grabbed a fork and handed one to Greg. "Most definitely."

Mike plated the eggplant parm beautifully, making sure to add some fresh chopped basil on top.

Dale took a bite. Then, another. "This is outstanding. Mike, you said your name is? What's your cooking experience?"

Mike smiled. "Glad you like it. I've worked all over the place from here to the city. I've even worked for Chef Ron."

Dale laughed. "What was that like?"

Mike chuckled back. "A bit rough but I survived, and I feel I'm better at what I do now. Ed, Jack, and I have been going over what Greg wants on the menu, and have made a few more dishes. Would you like to try those?"

Greg nodded enthusiastically. He was loving what they'd put together so far. It was exactly the style of cooking he'd envisioned in his restaurant.

After trying the other dishes, Greg and Dale headed down to the cellar for privacy away from the cooks, while Michael, Greg's son, lounged in a comfy spot on one of the wine cellar's plush couches playing video games.

Dale clapped his hands together. "OK, hear me out. I've got a crazy idea."

Greg shifted his eyes. "Uh, sure thing. How crazy are we talking?"

Dale leaned back in the chair and put his hands behind his head. "Hire Mike to be your chef. I could have him and the other cooks come do some training at my restaurant for a week or two. My guys could teach them a lot more."

Greg leaned forward. "You think he's chef material?"

Dale confidently smiled and nodded his head. "Yes, I do."

"What about Chef Ron? What do I tell him?"

Dale looked around. "He didn't show up for work today, correct? He dug his own grave. I'm telling you, I think this will work out nicely."

Greg reached across the table to Dale for a fist bump. "I literally feel like a weight has been lifted off my chest. Thank you for coming today."

Dale stood from the chair to go look at a crate of wine stacked nearby. "It is no problem at all. I'm happy to help—"

"Hey, guys," Liz's voice rang out. "I was wondering where you were. I should have figured you were in Greg's favorite part of the restaurant."

Greg greeted her with a kiss and a hug just as Donna stepped from behind Liz into plain sight. "I'm Donna, Liz's old friend from high school."

Liz smiled. "Yep, I was about to get to that. Dale, this is my friend, Donna. Greg, you remember Donna?"

Greg pivoted, smiling widely, to give Donna a hug and kiss on the cheek.

Dale's eyes widened and his heart beat faster as his eyes fell upon Donna. "It's very nice to meet you, Donna."

Eyes locked, Donna noted a distinct zing shot through her body. There seemed to be a mutual unspoken attraction between them, or was her mind playing tricks on her?

CHAPTER SIX

It was Memorial Day, a sunny eighty-three degrees, and absolutely gorgeous out. Cape May beaches were packed with beachgoers sprawled out on their towels or reclined in chairs reading books, swimming in the ocean, or simply enjoying the company of those with them while relaxing with their feet in the sand. The lifeguards whistled for swimmers to move closer to the designated swimming areas, and nearby, Bruce Springsteen could be heard playing from someone's radio. Canopies and brightly colored beach umbrellas littered the long stretch of sand in all directions. Coolers opened and closed as folks looked for a cold drink on this warm day. It surely was the quintessential Memorial Day weekend in New Jersey.

Across town, Donna prepared to meet Margaret, Liz, and Sarah for their first official beach day of the summer. She ran around packing her beach bag. Sunblock. *Check.* Sunglasses. *Check.* A bottle of water. *Check.* A book. *Check.* A beach towel. *Check.* Some snacks. *Check.* A Bluetooth speaker. *Check.* She had just about everything and a little time to spare. They weren't meeting for another forty-five minutes.

Donna fell back onto her bed, her big floppy sun hat falling forward onto her face. She closed her eyes for a second and then burst them open. The chest. She'd totally forgotten about the chest. She walked over to the closet and pulled the chest out again, setting it on the floor, when suddenly a lightbulb went off. She ran over to her sock drawer and felt around. Nothing. Disappointed, she sat back on the bed. She thought for a minute, and this time walked back to the sock drawer and emptied it. She knelt down, to get a good line of vision to the back of the drawer, and there, all the way in the back, a key was taped out of plain sight.

Donna grabbed the key, walked to the chest, and put the key into the lock. Sure enough, it unlocked. Upon opening, a strong smell of cedar and old papers wafted through the air. Donna's eyes lit up in anticipation of what she would find. She couldn't believe she didn't remember what she'd put inside. Then again, it had been over twenty years.

Donna's dad, Roy, appeared at her open door and chuckled. "You finally got that thing opened, eh?"

Donna smiled, pulling out a handful of papers. "This is my old guitar sheet music and handwritten lyrics. My gosh, I wrote so many songs back then. I was so full of creativity and confidence."

Roy crouched down next to Donna to inspect the music. "Well, you were always gifted. I taught you most of what I knew about guitar and music growing up, but you took it to another level. Remember when you won the school talent show playing the guitar? Your mother and I were so proud."

Donna sighed. "Yeah, I don't know what made me stop playing. I loved it so much. How could I have let it slip away from me like that?"

Roy gave Donna a comforting pat on the back and stood up. "I have something for you. I'll be right back."

After her dad left, Donna reached to the bottom of the chest, feeling a tiny notebook hit her fingers. She pulled it out and opened it. It was her old journal from high school. Donna opened to the first page and began reading, tears welling up in her eyes. She read a few more pages, before shutting it and sliding it into her beach bag.

Moments later, Roy appeared holding a guitar. "This is for you. I want you to have it. Back when you asked us to sell your guitar for you so you could have spending money at college … well we gave you the money you needed, but kept the guitar. It's been in the basement in its case all these years, and I'd completely forgotten about it."

Donna's eyes welled up again as she hugged her dad and then held her old guitar, the one that meant so much to her. "Dad, this is incredible. I can't believe you've had this this whole time."

Roy, smiled, feeling happy with himself. "Well, your mom was just going to sell it like you asked, but being a musician myself, I know how important it would be to you years later. I couldn't let it go."

Donna ran her fingers over the guitar, feeling the old strings. "I can't thank you enough."

Roy looked the guitar over. "I'll get some new strings on there and tune it right up for you. It'll be good as new. Just promise me you'll use it."

Donna sighed. "I don't know if I'll remember anything. It's been so long, Dad."

Roy thought for a moment. "You'll be surprised by what your fingers remember. It's muscle memory—like riding a bike. Once we learn how to ride a bike, we usually never forget."

Donna hugged her dad again before making her way to her bike to head off to the beach.

* * *

A few shore towns over, Judy and Bob were back at Corson's Inlet in Ocean City. Bob was getting better at fishing, and Judy was finally able to join him, though not to fish. Four-wheel drive vehicles were not allowed on the sand again until mid-

September, so they parked and walked this time. Bob was somewhat relieved about the prospect after the scary incident with his brother's truck getting stuck in the sand.

They found a secluded spot on the inlet and set up their beach chairs along the water. Bob got his fishing gear ready while Judy nestled into her chair with her sun hat and book, enjoying the quiet lapping of the water.

Bob finally got his rod baited and casted out into the water. He placed it in the rod holder in the sand, and sat in his chair next to Judy.

"You hungry? I made sandwiches," Bob said to Judy.

A look of surprise took over Judy's face. "You did?"

Bob chuckled. "Why are you so surprised?"

Judy went back to her book. "I don't know. I guess I'm used to being the one that prepares our lunches."

Bob reached into the cooler, grabbed two turkey-and-cheese sandwiches, and handed Judy one. "Well, while you were away on your scrapbooking weekend, I made sandwiches for my fishing trip with Dan. He loved the sandwich, which made me proud that I made something not only edible but enjoyable. So, that's my new thing now—making sandwiches."

Judy laughed and opened the sandwich out of the plastic wrap and put it on her lap. She held the sandwich up to inspect it. "What's all in here, dear?"

Bob held his sandwich and looked at it. "Well, it's fresh turkey breast, American cheese, fresh sliced tomato, iceberg lettuce, mayo, and some bacon."

Judy took a bite and swallowed. "This *is* fantastic. We may have to put you on lunch duty from here on out."

Bob reached back into another bag. "I also got us some kettle chips and some crispy green grapes. I think this will hold us through most of the day."

"Well, it seems my weekend away did us both some good. We each got a sense of a little more independence, which I think is great," Judy said as she went back to her book.

Moments later, dogs belonging to a nearby couple started barking and playing near the waterline. The dogs rumbled and tumbled in the sand while a woman threw them a tennis ball. After more playing, the dogs eventually walked back to their owner's chairs, sitting beside them happily in the sand, trying to get shade under the umbrella. The woman filled two bowls with water from a large jug and placed them in front of the dogs. Both eagerly lapped it up before gently taking a proffered treat from her hand.

"Bob, look at how joyous those dogs are. I didn't know dogs were allowed on this beach," Judy said pointing.

Bob glanced over at the dogs and sighed, feeling a tinge of envy. "I don't think they're allowed this time of year. I do miss having a dog though. It hasn't been the same since our Brutus passed five years ago."

Judy smiled and put her hand on Bob's shoulder. "Brutus had a wonderful, long life. I miss him too."

Bob looked back at the dogs relaxing in the sand. "Why don't we take a drive to the local shelter one of these days. No pressure. Just maybe take a look around."

Judy closed her book. "Hon, I really don't want another dog. They're so much work. If we want to travel again, who'd watch the dog? We'd have to rush home from wherever we go to let the dog outside to go to the bathroom. It just doesn't sound appealing to me right now."

Bob sighed, sadness creeping in his eyes. "I just think the joy they bring into our lives outweighs all of that. Not to mention, there are ways to work around things. For instance, hiring a dog walker, bringing the dog with us when we travel or even seeing Margaret or Liz or another family member or friend would take the dog in while we travel."

Judy looked over at Bob, feeling her heart ache a little for him. "We'll see."

Bob smiled slightly on the inside. That had been the closest

Judy had come to agreeing to another dog. He'd take what he could get at this point.

Judy looked down the beach and out of the corner of her eye saw an area with lots of shells. "I think I'm going to go do some shelling now. My girlfriends are very into shelling, and I've always wanted to try to do it seriously."

Bob nodded and got up abruptly to see what was biting on his line. "Find me something nice, dear."

Judy smiled while finishing the last bite of her sandwich and grabbed the canvas bag she'd brought to collect shells. They were situated more on the marshy inlet side, but up a ways, the ocean side had a lot of good shells. She walked down the beach, passing tall grasses and hundreds of tiny fiddler crabs scurrying across the beach. She moved to the side, careful not to step on them as they hurried into their little burrows in the sand. The water was calm on the inlet side, the current only causing soft, gentle lapping unless the occasional boat or jet ski passed through. Judy walked towards the water, wanting to get her feet wet. She passed other folks enjoying the day in their chairs, smiling and nodding at them until she finally got to the area where the good seashells would be. Back where Bob was fishing, it was all just hundreds of clam shells. She was looking for something more unique.

It was low-to-mid tide, which was perfect for shelling. She kept at the water's edge, stopping every few feet to inspect a cluster of shells. After ten minutes, she spotted a few intact moon shells and promptly dunked them into the ocean to get the sand off before putting them gently in her bag. When she looked back up, about ten feet ahead, she squinted to see if she was imagining things. There, sitting by itself with only foaming ocean water surrounding it, was a pristine whelk shell. She had never seen one out in the wild before, only broken pieces and remnants of them.

Drawn to it, Judy scooped it up and in the process of squatting down, nearly bumped into a woman trying to do the same.

"Oh, sorry there. I didn't see you. I had my eye on this beautiful whelk shell," she said, holding it up.

The lady scoffed, holding a bag full of shells in her hand. "I've never seen you before. Do you usually shell here?"

Judy, oblivious to the woman's rudeness, smiled. "Nope. Never. It's my first time here. It's really my first adventure shelling too."

The lady squinted and put her hand on her hip. "Well, this is *my* shelling area. I've lived here my entire life, and this is my secret spot. I don't want anyone ruining that for me."

Judy, finally realizing this woman wasn't too happy with her, put her whelk shell in her canvas bag. "Well, do you own this beach? As far as I know it's public."

The lady's face turned red in frustration, and she marched away in the other direction.

Judy shook it off. She wasn't going to let this stranger ruin her otherwise wonderful day. As she walked back to Bob, still searching for shells along the way, she spotted something blue that had just been pushed out of the ocean. Her girlfriends had told her to keep an eye out for sea glass; it was highly coveted among shellers. And there, just waiting to be plucked up, laid pieces of blue and green sea glass.

Giddy with excitement now, Judy trotted back to Bob, who had just hooked a little fish and thrown it back. "You won't believe what I found. Just look at all of these goodies," Judy said while pulling her treasures out of the bag.

Bob glanced over, perplexed by her fascination with shells but happy to see Judy thrilled. "Very nice, hon. What are you going to do with them?"

Judy inspected her shells and sea glass closely. "I'm going to craft with the sea glass and display the others around our flower beds. It will be lovely—quite lovelier than the woman I ran into who was mad about me shelling in her supposed territory."

Bob chuckled. "A throw down with seashellers. I've heard it all."

Judy applied some lotion, nestled back into her chair, stretching her legs as far into the sand as possible, and closed her eyes. "You know, I could get used to this. When are we coming here again? How about tomorrow?"

Bob laughed. "We'll see."

* * *

Back on the Cape May's Cove Beach, Margaret, Liz, Sarah, Donna, and the kids had gotten their little area of the beach set up. A canopy, two umbrellas, a cooler station, a couple of sheets spread out for the kids, a sand toy area, and of course, their chairs.

They slathered on lotion, settled into their chairs, which all faced each other so they could talk but still see the kids, and sipped on their cold drinks. Bon Jovi played loudly on someone's radio in the distance, and for what seemed like miles, all you could see were brightly colored umbrellas and people.

Margaret laughed. "It's funny. So many visitors look at our crowded beaches and roll their eyes, but I have to say, growing up here, I'm accustomed to it. In a way, I like it. It feels like one big beach party, and it provides plenty of good people watching. Not to mention, our kids always find other kids to play with here."

Liz motioned to the ocean. "Yep. Look, they've already found friends in the ocean. They're boogie boarding with some right now."

Donna smiled and reached into her beach bag, pulling out her old journal. "Guess what I found at my parents'. My old guitar music and my journal from high school. It's caused so many feelings to come rushing back."

Sarah took a sip of her drink. "That is so neat. Do you still play the guitar? I remember how good you were. You blew away all those guys playing guitar at that talent show, remember?"

Donna laughed. "Oh, I remember. I'm being flooded with memories lately. But no, I haven't played guitar in ages."

Margaret furrowed her brow. "So, why do you think you stopped? Did you grow out of it? Were you no longer interested in it anymore?"

Donna leafed through her journal. "Honestly, I couldn't remember why. However, after reading some of this journal, I'm realizing that I threw away my dreams for Adam's dreams. He wanted to go away to college in California and he convinced me to go too. I was in love, so being with him was top priority. Then, when he got into law school, I was the one supporting us—I had no time for hobbies or advancing my career. I had ambitions of chasing a music career, but it's such a hard industry to break into. It takes a lot of work and dedication. Instead, I took an office job that made me absolutely miserable to keep us afloat."

Liz shook her head. "Once he became a lawyer, was it easier?"

Donna sighed. "Not really. By then, I just didn't have that burning passion anymore for playing music. I let it all go. I worked my way up in ranks at that miserable office job, but it never was the plan … and now I'm forty-five. It's too late now."

Sarah cocked her head to the side and stared at Donna. "Too late? Are you kidding? I just started my own business just this year. I'm the same age as you. Margaret and Liz just started running a B&B business last year, and Liz's husband is in the process of opening his own restaurant. Do not give me that excuse. If anything, now seems like a perfect time to start anew."

Margaret and Liz nodded. "She's right."

Donna thought for a moment. "That's the thing. I don't know what I want. How does one make a living playing music these days unless you make it big? I don't want to play in a cover band every weekend, that's for sure. Not to mention, I haven't played in twenty years. It's not the same. Maybe my dream is something else, something bigger, something that encompasses more than a career. I'm hoping to discover that while I get myself together in Cape May."

Just then, Sarah received a call and she looked down to see it was Mark. "Oh no. Oh, no, no."

Donna, Margaret, and Liz all looked over at her. "What? Is everything OK?"

Sarah let the call go to voice mail, then saw the new message alert pop up. "I guess I forgot to tell you guys. Mark called me a couple of weeks ago while I was out with Chris on the boat. We haven't spoken since the breakup back in February. I never called him back, but he just called again."

Margaret's eyes widened. "Well, this is interesting. What could he possibly want?"

Sarah held the phone up to her ear and listened to the voice mail.

"Hey, Sarah. It's Mark again. I know I called you already, and I guess you don't want to talk to me. I'm just looking for someone to talk to, I presume. My mom just passed unexpectedly. I don't know who to turn to."

Sarah put the phone back in her bag. "Well, the first time he called, he asked about hanging out. This time, it seems he just wants a friend. His mother passed. I don't know what to do, guys? Do I go see him?"

Liz scratched her forehead and thought. "It really comes down to this. Do you *want* to see him?"

CHAPTER SEVEN

The next day, Greg sat at a table in his restaurant with Mike, his newly appointed chef, and the two head cooks, Jack and Ed. Sipping hot coffee that Greg had picked up from Sarah's coffeehouse, they each looked at the mock menu Greg had designed.

"So, what do you guys think of the menu? Doable?" Greg asked, looking around the table.

Jack nodded. "I think so, but we will need more kitchen help."

Greg took a gulp of his coffee. "Yep. I'm on that. Working on the rest of the kitchen staff, server and host staff, all of it. However, right now, I really want to nail this menu. Any thoughts or concerns with it?"

Mike rubbed his chin. "Well, not really. Everything looks pretty straightforward, but will you be changing the offerings every so often?"

Greg smiled. "Well, sort of. What I really want is to have a different specials menu every week. The best part is I'm going to let you guys head that menu. We'll sit down for a meeting once a week and let our imaginations run wild with what to put on the following week's specials menu. I'll run out and get the ingredients, then we'll create them and taste test them before making our final decision."

Ed's eyes widened. "That actually sounds great."

Greg took his last gulp of coffee, stood up from his chair and put his sunglasses on. "Perfect. Well, how about we do some group grocery shopping and grab whatever's left to get on the existing menu. Maybe we can try out some specials ideas if there's time. I think it will be fun."

The guys happily got up, pushed their chairs in, and slipped off their chef's attire, then followed Greg to the car.

Ten minutes later, they were at Greg's favorite grocery store.

Greg grabbed a cart. "OK, follow me. I know where the best of the best is in this store. Maybe we can experiment."

Ed eyed some fresh, locally grown peas and spinach and grabbed bags of them. "OK, locally sourced fresh produce is the name of the game. We have to get these."

Greg smiled, feeling giddy. "I like where your head is at. Throw them in the cart."

Mike grabbed some locally grown baby beets and butter crunch lettuce. "How about these?"

"Perfect! I'm really starting to think that I want to revolve the menu, and particularly the specials menu, around fresh, locally sourced items. You know, farm to table? Nothing tastes better than coming straight off the farm," Greg said, his mind swirling with ideas.

The guys nodded in confident agreement before glancing around the store for more items.

Bunches of newly picked red rhubarb caught Jack's eye. "I think I've got a dessert idea with that rhubarb over there."

Greg clapped his hands together. "Oh, I can't wait to try that, Jack."

After spending another half hour in the grocery store, they

excitedly packed the car full with grocery bags and headed back to the restaurant to start cooking.

They followed each other up the steps to the front door of the restaurant. Greg turned the doorknob, opening the door a crack. "That's weird. Did someone forget to lock the door behind them?"

Jack raised his hand to grab Greg's attention. "Nope. I was the last out, and I locked up. I even double checked the door to make sure it was locked."

Greg furrowed his brow, opening the door wider, and peering inside before spotting someone in the kitchen.

"Who's there?" Greg bellowed from the front door, the guys peering behind him over his shoulder.

There wasn't an answer, but pots and pans were definitely clanging loudly.

Greg walked in, set down the grocery bag in his hands onto a nearby table, and marched towards the kitchen. "Chef Ron? What are you doing here?"

Ron stopped making noise and gave a nervous smile. "I'm reporting to work."

Greg shook his head. "No. You were a no-call, no-show for over a week, and now you think you can waltz back in? I already have a new chef."

Ron walked out from the kitchen and laughed. "A new chef? Who could you have possibly hired?"

Mike cleared his throat, feeling slightly less confident. "Me."

Ron laughed again. "You? You don't have any experience as a chef, do you? You've only ever been a line cook."

Greg sternly interrupted. "Yes, Mike is the new chef—he has what it takes. I've tasted what he's cooked and it not only matches the style of food I want—a fact that you disregarded —but it was absolutely delicious. He's got what it takes, and he's also enjoyable to work with, which cannot be said about you."

Ron sank down into a nearby chair, confidence and energy draining out of him. "I don't know what to say. It's been rough these past months, years even."

Ed, Jack, and Mike quickly made themselves useful by grabbing the groceries and hurrying into the kitchen. They did not want to get involved, though they still wanted to listen in.

Greg took a seat across from Ron, letting out a big sigh. "What's going on, Ron?"

Ron looked out a nearby window at the people walking by. "My wife left me. She took the kids. She's staying at her parents' house. She won't talk to me. My life is in shambles. All I had left was my job, and I even screwed that up."

Greg shook his head, his lighthearted excitement from earlier in the day turned heavy. "I'm so sorry. It looks like you have a lot to think about. I don't know your situation, but perhaps talking to someone close to you could help. A friend? A relative?"

Ron cradled his head in his hands. "Those are the last people I want to know about my screw ups. It's much easier telling someone I'm not close to. I just feel like a failure."

Greg looked towards the kitchen, motioning to Ed. "How about a coffee, Ron? Maybe we can start there."

Ron made a little smile. "Thank you."

Minutes later, Ed brought out a coffee from the back, placing it in front of Ron. "Thank you, Ed," Ron said, appreciation and sadness showing in his eyes.

Greg looked back at Ron. "You don't have to talk about it if you don't want, but is there any way for you to salvage your marriage?"

Ron gently took a sip of his coffee. "Yeah. Marriage counseling. When I refused, she stormed out with the kids. I guess I didn't want to admit that we had issues. I wanted to believe everything was fine. Counseling is just not for me. I've always worked my own problems out."

Greg nodded. "I understand that, but I'm going to interject

my opinion here. If you truly want to save your marriage, I recommend doing the marriage counseling."

Ron paused. "You're right. I have to see someone about my anger and stress issues. I know I have them. It's ruined countless jobs in the past. My only saving grace is that I'm a great a chef. Speaking of which, I guess I have to find a new job."

Just then, Mike, Ed, and Jack brought out some dishes they'd quickly whipped up in the kitchen, setting them on the table in front of Greg and Ron.

"We thought we could all taste these together. We'd like your input," Mike said, looking at Ron and Greg.

As much as Mike had hated working with Chef Ron, he respected his culinary craft and opinion.

Greg and Ron's faces lit up, as they were both pretty hungry, but what really stuck out to them was how beautifully plated the dishes were; how fresh and vibrant they looked.

Greg and Ron took bites out of what looked like a different play on bruschetta, it had ricotta, lemon, and basil.

With the other cooks standing behind him, Mike cleared his throat. "Now, before you say anything, let me say this. Greg, I know you like to keep the rustic original Italian dishes, but there's something to be said about some slight experimentations to keep the customers on their toes. It's somewhat like what Ron was doing, but I played it down more, so it would be more appealing to your customers."

Ron finished his piece and quickly grabbed another, scarfing it down. Greg was too busy chewing to get words out for a few moments, then a big smile appeared on his face. "You knocked this out of the park. It has familiar old Italian flavors with the ricotta and basil, and the lemon and honey took it that extra mile. This is fantastic."

Ron nodded while still chewing. "This is wonderful. Who spearheaded this one?"

Mike smiled, feeling proud of himself. "This one was my idea."

Ron, looked over at Mike, bewilderment in his eyes. "How come you never spoke up with menu ideas in the past when I've worked with you?"

Mike looked down at the floor. "I don't know. You didn't seem to want to hear anyone's ideas, and I didn't want to step on your toes. You can be pretty intimidating and not the easiest to work with, Chef Ron."

Ron let out a sigh, and hopped out of his chair. "You're right. I need to make a change, both for my personal and professional life."

* * *

It was a few hours to sunset and Margaret decided to schedule a beach meetup with Liz, Sarah, Donna, Chris, Dave, and the kids. The perfect spot was directly across the street from Dave's and Chris's houses.

Margaret turned up first at the beach with Abby and Harper and set out some chairs. Walking to the water's edge, she gauged the temperature—still brutally cold, which was to be expected for early June.

Dave, Donna, Liz and her boys each arrived separately shortly after, positioning their chairs and blankets on the now mostly empty beach since the throng of beachgoers from earlier had packed up and gone home. Liz's boys immediately ran over to play with their cousins, making the sisters smile over their kids' close bond.

Margaret sat in her chair and pulled a long-sleeved shirt over her head. "I feel like we're waiting for a movie to start, but instead it's the sunset. Sarah and Chris said they'll be here shortly, by the way."

Dave looked over and smiled at Margaret, lovingly brushing a stray hair off her face, then stood up. "I'm going to go see what the kids found over there by the water. It looks like a horseshoe crab."

Margaret grabbed Dave's hand affectionately. "Have fun!"

Liz smiled at Margaret and Dave's public display of affection. "Greg said he'll stop by after he's done at the restaurant."

"How's the restaurant going? I can't wait to go and eat," Margaret said excitedly.

Liz let out a deep sigh. "He's having all sorts of drama over there. I'm starting to wonder if this was a good idea. He seems to be handling it, though. Dale—his friend who owns that restaurant in Collingswood—has been coming around more to help, which has been wonderful."

Donna sat upright in her chair. "Dale? The guy who was there when I went to the restaurant with you? How does he know him … out of curiosity?"

"They're old college buddies. Dale is a cool guy. He's just been through a lot over the last few years."

Donna pried, "Really? How so?"

"Well, he went through a nasty divorce a few years ago that shattered him. Then, he met someone wonderful a year later, and they dated for a year, but she broke his heart and he's been quite … different since," Liz said.

Margaret furrowed her brow. "Different? How?"

Liz laughed. "Well, he's become quite a—"

Just then, Greg snuck up behind Liz, putting his hands on her shoulders and scaring the life out of her.

Liz yelped. "Greg! Don't do that. You know my heart can't take it."

Greg laughed as Dale walked up next to him. "Hey, guys. This is my friend, Dale. He stopped by the restaurant, and I invited him to our soiree on the beach you've all got going."

Dale put his hand up in greeting while looking around at everyone before his eyes locked on Donna's again.

Donna's heart skipped a beat. She'd been hoping she would see Dale again.

Margaret pointed to some vacant chairs. "Here, take a seat

in those. I brought them for the girls, but they aren't going to use them."

Greg nodded. "Thank you. We'll take you up on that, but first we have to walk a block back that way. We passed an old college buddy we wanted to say hello to. We'll be right back."

Dale waved politely again at everyone as they walked away, his eyes lingering on Donna once more.

Moments later, Sarah and Chris arrived, and Liz extended her hand to Chris. "I'm Liz, Sarah's friend. And this our friend Donna."

Donna smiled and waved hello.

Sarah sighed, joking, "You beat me to introductions."

Chris smiled. "Nice to meet you, Liz and Donna, and good to see you again, Margaret. What do you think of this beach? It's perfect, isn't it? I love having it directly across the street from my house. It's not ideal for swimming, but perfect for just enjoying the day or watching the sunset."

"It's absolutely wonderful. No need to look for a parking spot or walk far. You've got everything you need," Margaret said, looking over at the kids and Dave examining whatever sea creatures they'd found.

Sarah piped in, "Chris owns the Blue Heron Birding Boat. You have to come sometime. It's so wonderful."

Just then, Chris's phone rang, and when he looked at it, his eyes widened. "Sorry to interrupt the conversation, but I have to step away and take this."

Chris walked away to answer it, and Sarah's happy expression immediately vanished.

Liz took one look at Sarah and knew something was up. "Are you OK? What's going on?"

Sarah looked over at Chris, who was a good distance away. "I'm almost positive that phone call is his ex-wife. They share a son together, Sam. She calls him constantly. Like five or more times a day. Anytime we do anything or go anywhere lately, she calls."

Donna's eye widened. "Why?"

Sarah shrugged. "At first I thought it was to talk about Sam or coordinate pick-ups, but then I realized that doesn't take five phone calls a day. I'm not sure, but I know he doesn't like it."

Margaret shook her head. "That doesn't sound good. Can he tell her to stop? Set some boundaries with her?"

Sarah sighed. "I think he's afraid to. He loves Sam, and I bet he's worried it would jeopardize his time with him. He's going to have to buckle down and do something soon, though. It's going to affect our relationship sooner or later. I went from dating Mark, who was barely ever around due to traveling for work, to Chris, whose days are constantly being interrupted with phone calls from his ex. Speaking of Mark, I never did call him back. I'm thinking I should."

Liz bit her lip. "Are you sure that's a good idea?"

Sarah glanced at Chris. Still on the phone, he motioned that he was heading back to the house for a minute. Sarah pursed her lips. "I don't know. You know what? I'm going to bite the bullet and call him now." She pushed up out of her chair and walked down the shoreline, her stomach tying in knots as she pulled out her cell phone and dialed Mark's number.

He picked up immediately, as though he'd been waiting for her to call. "Hey, Sarah. How are you?"

Sarah looked out towards the ocean. "I'm fine. How are you? I'm so sorry to hear about your mother."

"Thank you, I appreciate it. Would you maybe want to meet for lunch or something sometime? To … talk?" Marked asked.

Sarah hesitated. "Look, Mark—"

Mark interrupted. "As friends. No pressure. I just really need someone to talk to."

Sarah sighed. "OK. That could work."

Mark's voice lifted. "Perfect. How about in a couple days around noon? At our old favorite spot."

"That works for me. See you then," Sarah said. Hanging up, she looked over at their group on the beach to see Chris walking back from the house.

Greg and Dale were also back, and Dale choose the chair closest to Donna.

Dale looked over at Donna. "Hey. I think we met at the restaurant recently."

Donna felt slight butterflies and insecurity at the same time. "That's right. I hear you have a restaurant in Collingswood."

Dale angled his chair so he could see Donna's face better, bumping her knee with his in the process, causing goose bumps to erupt over his skin. "Yes, I do. Have you ever been there?"

Donna shook her head. "Actually, no. This is my first time back to New Jersey in years. I lived in California for … a while."

Dale furrowed his brow. "What brought you back?"

Donna gulped. "I'm going through a divorce. I kind of wanted to move back and get my bearings before figuring out what the next step is for me."

Dale's eyes flashed with understanding. "I've been through one myself."

Donna nodded and took a sip of her drink. She felt guilty already knowing that since Liz had just told her.

Dale looked towards the ocean then back at Donna, their eyes lingering on each other again. "So … um … this is going to seem a little off the wall, but what are you doing tomorrow?"

Donna felt a blush rise on her cheeks. "Tomorrow? I don't think I have much going on. Why?"

Dale pushed his foot into the sand. "Well, you see, I have these Phillies tickets. My brother was supposed to join me, and Greg, he's not a baseball guy. Would you want to go? They're great seats."

Donna laughed. "You mean like a date?"

Dale paused, his heart racing. "I guess you could say that."

Donna looked around at everyone else talking with each other, oblivious to what was going on with her and Dale. "I think I'd like that."

CHAPTER EIGHT

"This spot is perfect," Judy said as she set up her beach chair and dropped her beach bag onto the sand.

Bob had already kneeled in the sand, working on setting up the beach umbrella. "We forgot our sand anchor. Hopefully it doesn't get too windy and it stays put."

Judy nestled into her chair and looked at the sun's peaceful reflection on the water. "I could get used to this. You've got me hooked on coming to Corson's Inlet, dear."

Bob finished with the umbrella and stood up to get his fishing rod situated. "I'm a little hooked myself, pun intended. Maybe I'll actually catch a good one today."

Judy looked around, then stood up. "You know, there's a little hiking area right over there. I think I'm going to go explore."

Bob baited his hook, casting his line before looking to where his wife pointed. Securing the rod in the pole stand in in the sand, he sat in his chair. "That sounds like fun. Maybe I'll join you next time before I have to watch my rod."

Judy put her shoes on and made her way to the wooded walking area that was full of trees and nature right along the water. After walking down the sandy path for a bit, she stopped to admire the way the sun peaked through the trees, casting different angles of glow along the leaves. She took a deep breath, savoring the moment, before opening her eyes, looking down, and screaming.

"Ahhhhh!"

A man about eight feet in front of her on the trail stopped in his tracks. "Are you OK, ma'am?"

Judy just pointed, unable to utter any words. Slithering across the sand, a somewhat large black snake made its way quickly across the walkway and back into the brush.

"Oh he's harmless, I assure you. No need to be scared. I think he's more scared of you than you are of him, to be honest," the man said as he slowly made his way around Judy to see where the snake had gone.

Judy laughed. "Can you believe I've never seen a snake in the wild? I'm terrified of them. I think my heart just jumped out of my chest and ran down the street."

The man laughed. "I totally get it. They give me the creeps too, but it's nice to be educated about them. They truly are fascinating creatures. Well, enjoy the rest of your walk. Hopefully you won't come across anymore surprise visitors."

Judy sighed, waved goodbye, and continued walking the trail. She thought about how she needed to get out in nature more—how had she never seen a snake in the wild before?

She finally made her way out of the trees and brush to where the trail ended at the beach and ocean. She took off her shoes to walk closer to the dunes this time instead of the water. She could look for shells on her way back, but she wanted to see what this part of the beach had to offer on her way back to Bob.

Judy noticed small, three-inch holes all over the sand as she walked. She had bent down to study one when something caught her eye. A small crab emerged, walking sideways away from Judy. It had little black eyes atop its head and, quite frankly, was a lot less scary than the snake she'd just seen.

"Do you live in this hole?" Judy asked the crab that wanted nothing to do with her. It just watched her, waiting to see which direction it needed to move in order to stay away.

A few more crabs scurried across the beach then ran back into their holes after seeing Judy.

Judy smiled. "OK, I'll leave you alone. Nice real estate you've got here right on the beach. Must be nice."

She made her way back to Bob, who had just caught a flounder.

"Wow. What a catch!" Judy said as she approached.

Bob grabbed his yardstick and measured it. "Yep, but too small to keep. I've gotta throw it back. How was your walk?"

Judy laughed. "Well, I ran into a large black snake that nearly gave me a heart attack, and then I saw crabs all over the beach. It was truly an enlightening walk about the nature around here."

Bob unhooked the flounder and threw it back. "Those crabs are called ghost crabs. Neat, aren't they?"

Judy got comfortable in her chair and opened her book. "It was a great walk. Now I want to get a book that tells me about all of these creatures. For now, this fiction book will do."

Bob prepped his fishing rod with new bait before sitting in his chair next to Judy, this time closing his eyes. The gentle lapping of water and seagulls and shorebird calls in the distance put him to sleep.

Judy looked over at Bob from her book and smiled. Taking a cue from him, she got settled for a little cat nap. She shut her eyes and let the beach sounds lull her to sleep, expecting to rest her eyes and meditate.

An hour later, with the sun searing their skin, they both woke up abruptly. Two dogs—lost ones, not strays—were happily licking their arms, expecting some affection in return.

Bob nearly fell out of his chair out of disarray. "What? Who's there? What's going on?"

Judy shielded the sun from her eyes. "I think we fell

asleep … but how long has it been? And where's our umbrella?"

Bob, realizing the umbrella was missing, looked down the beach. "I haven't a clue, it must have blown away while we were napping."

Judy looked down at her arms. "I'm toasted to a crisp. I think sunburned is putting it lightly. I look like a lobster."

Bob looked at his arms. "I'm also a lobster now. I guess we forgot to apply sunblock."

Judy nodded. "And we forgot the umbrella sand anchor, which didn't help matters. Come on, we have to go find it and make sure it didn't impale anyone."

Bob helped Judy out of her seat and they headed in the direction the wind was blowing.

"I think I see it up ahead," Judy said.

When they came upon a woman sunbathing with their umbrella still fully open and laying in the sand next to her, Judy cleared her throat. "Hi, there. So sorry. Our umbrella got away from us."

The woman moved her sunglasses down the bridge of her nose and looked up. "Oh you shoobies need to find another beach."

Bob's eyes widened as he knew Judy was about to be set off.

"*Shoobies?* I'll have you know, we're from the Jersey Shore. Full-time residents! We are not shoobies, but even if we were, we'd have every right to be on this public beach too," Judy said as she grabbed the umbrella.

The woman sat up. "Weren't you the one shelling on this beach? You took that whelk shell right as I was trying to get it."

Judy rolled her eyes. "Yes, that was me, but I didn't see you until I already had it in hand."

The woman shook her head and laid back on her towel. "Well, I'm sick of shoobies, and I'm sick of everyone finding my secret beach spots. Pretty soon Corson's Inlet is going to be a circus. There won't be one spot on this beach to put a chair. You watch."

Judy sighed. "Come on, Bob. Let's get back to our chairs. I don't have time for rude people."

Bob chuckled, trying to make light of the situation and followed behind Judy.

After they were out of earshot, Judy took Bob's hand, holding it tightly. "Can you believe the nerve of that woman? She's the one I told you about when I went shelling that one day. She thinks she owns this beach."

Bob shrugged. "Well … no, she wasn't nice about it, but I get it. I remember when our favorite secluded beach in Cape May became a hot spot. We went from having it to ourselves every day to having hundreds of people bumping up against us, leaving trash and litter everywhere. We have to learn to share while being respectful of both others and the beach."

Judy squeezed his hand harder before planting a kiss on his cheek. "You always have a way of looking at things from a positive angle."

* * *

"Hey, there. I see you're ready for the ball game," Dale said as Donna hopped in his car decked out in red-and-white Phillies attire and holding a baseball glove.

Donna laughed. "Yeah, I ran out and bought a Phillies shirt and hat. I haven't been to a baseball game in forever. I used to love going growing up."

Dale smiled and winked. "Well, I'm sure we'll have fun."

Donna adjusted her red baseball cap and tried to shake her jitters.

"You OK over there?" Dale said as he drove the car.

Donna took a deep breath. "Yeah, I think so. I guess I'm just a little nervous. I haven't been on a date in a long time. Adam was my high school sweetheart."

They came up to a stop sign, and Dale looked over at Donna, his eyes once again lingering, causing a zing to go through Donna's body. "I get it. No pressure. Let's just go enjoy ourselves. We do have an hour and half to get to know each other in the car, though."

Donna laughed. "What do you want to know?"

Dale thought for a moment. "Why are you getting a divorce?"

Donna sighed, having not really discussed it much since moving back to Cape May. "I wasn't happy anymore. We didn't have many friends out in California. Adam was a lawyer and was always working. I wasn't crazy about my job, and I guess I realized I wanted more. I tried to get Adam to go along with the idea of making some changes, but he *was* happy. He liked working eighteen-hour days and being on call when he wasn't working. His job was his life. So, I left. What about you?"

Dale gulped. "My wife left me for someone else. It took me a while to get over it and move on. It cut like a knife. Then, I eventually moved on and met someone else, but that situation didn't work out either. Since then, I've been a free bird. I try to get out more."

They spent the rest of the car ride divulging their heart's desires, interests, and fears and getting to know each other more deeply.

When Dale stopped at a red light near the stadium, he casted his gaze back on Donna. "Since you weren't happy in California, what do you think *would* make you happy?"

Donna watched some fans walking on the street towards the stadium, full of energy and excitement. "I guess I want someone to spend time with. I want to be near family and friends more. I want a cozy cottage—with or without a white picket fence is to be determined. I want a dog that greets me with a wagging tail when I get home. I want big family meals and walks on the beach. I want a job that's fulfilling but isn't my life. I want to ride bikes at sunset on a whim to the beach, and strum my guitar to the sounds of the ocean. There's a lot I want, Dale."

Dale nodded, a wide grin appearing on his face as his eyes locked on Donna's. "That was extraordinary. I love everything you just said. You just made me want some things I didn't know I wanted. I have to ask, though. You play guitar?"

Donna smiled. "It's a long story, but I used to play guitar and stopped after I moved to California for college, which was eons ago. It turns out, my dad saved my guitar from high school, but I haven't strummed one since then. I'm both curious and afraid of what I have or haven't retained in my mind."

Dale's heart fluttered in excitement. "Did Liz or Greg happen to mention to you that I play guitar?"

Donna smiled and shook her head. "No. Never. You do?"

Dale laughed. "Yep. I have a group of friends who each play one instrument or another, and we get together every Thursday night for a jam session. In the summer, we put on some shows here or there. All original music. It's so much fun. You should come join in sometime."

Donna laughed. "But I haven't picked a guitar up in twenty-five years or more. I feel like I'd make a fool of myself."

"I think you'll do just fine. Just come sometime," Dale said as he pulled into the stadium's parking lot.

They got out, walked to the stadium, handed in their tickets, and made their way to their seats.

"OK, this is our section here," Dale said, eyeing the tickets.

Donna followed him all the way to the very front near the third baseline. "*These* are our seats? I can practically touch the field we're so close. This is awesome!"

Dale laughed. "I have season tickets. I wanted to surprise you with how good they were. Would you like to grab some hot dogs and drinks?"

Donna nodded and followed him back up the stairs to the

inside corridor of the stadium where all of the vendors were. Dale reached back and grabbed her hand as a bunch of people tried to squeeze by them on the steps to get to their seats.

They finally made their way to the corridor before Dale spotted his favorite hot dog stand. "There's Joe. He's been running that hot dog cart for years now. Good guy. You like hot dogs?"

Donna laughed. "They're OK, but since I'm at a ball game, I probably should have one."

Dale walked over to Joe, said his hellos, and was handed two hot dogs. Passing one to Donna, he said, "The condiments are over there if you want any."

Donna added mustard and took a bite of the hot dog while the announcer came on over the loudspeaker. "I never knew a hot dog could taste so good. Why does this taste different than the rest?"

Dale laughed. "Because there's nothing like a hot dog at a ball game. The nostalgia, the clink of the ball when it hits the bat, the happy fans, the traditions of the old game ... it hits you right in the heart. It's why I love coming here so much."

After snagging some drinks and walking around a little more, they made their way back to their seats in time for the start of the game.

One of the Phillies had a base hit, which prompted Dale to jump out of his seat along with a ton of other people in the stands around them.

"Good hit!" Dale said as he clapped and smiled.

Just then, a worker carrying a tray of water ice came walking down the steps. "Water ice! Get your water ice! Get your water ice!"

Dale sat back down, and pulled out his wallet. "Do you like water ice?"

"I sure do," Donna said joyfully.

Dale held his hand up to the guy selling water ice, who

promptly came towards them. "I'll take two lemon water ices or *wooder* ices, as we pronounce it in Jersey."

The guy handed each of them a water ice before moving along.

Donna scooped some lemon water ice into her mouth and casted her eyes back on the game in the nick of time. Seemingly all at once, she heard the crack of the bat and instinctively knew the ball was headed their way. Reflexively, her left hand slid into the glove perched on her thigh, and Donna jumped out of her seat just in time to catch the foul ball that hurtled straight at them.

Dale looked over in astonishment, while fans all around them cheered for Donna. "Did you really just catch that foul ball while still holding your water ice? I'm impressed."

Donna laughed, full of adrenaline. "I guess my brain can retain old things—I haven't caught a ball since high school either."

After spending a few hours enjoying the game, they happily walked back to the car.

Dale grazed his hand next to Donna's. "What are you doing the rest of the day? Anything going on?"

Donna thought for a moment. "No, I don't have any set plans. You?"

Dale smiled. "How about we stop at Porridge, my restaurant, in Collingwood on the way back to Cape May? I can get us some counter seating in the back."

"That sounds perfect."

Dale clapped his hands. "Awesome. First, I need to stop somewhere."

They hopped back into the car and drove off to Collingswood where Dale parked on a little street full of quaint shops.

"I'll be right back. Wait here," he said with a smile as he hopped out of the car.

Five minutes later, Dale walked out with a fresh bouquet of sunflowers wrapped in newspaper.

"These are for you," he said as he handed them to Donna.

"Are you serious? They are beautiful. That's why you wanted to stop?"

Dale smiled and shrugged. "I just felt the urge to get the beautiful girl sitting next to me something beautiful."

Donna's heart leapt in her chest, a feeling she hadn't felt since first meeting Adam.

CHAPTER NINE

"Harper and Abby, can you hand me that small board to the left there?" Dave asked.

Harper and Abby nodded and grabbed the board as fast as they could, working together to hold it up so Dave could reach from the tree.

Margaret approached with a basket of zucchini, cucumbers, and herbs. "I thought you girls were helping me harvest from the garden today. What happened?"

Abby looked up at Dave in the tree. "We kind of decided we'd rather help Dave build the tree house."

Dave laughed as he nailed another board on the platform. "I think they're a little excited about this tree house. Can't say I blame them. It was one of my favorite things when I was their age."

Harper grabbed her mother's hand. "We want to show you something we found over by the creek."

Margaret set her basket down and let Abby and Harper lead her to the nearby creek where an eight-by-eight-foot patch of cleared ground sat full of sunlight among the many trees.

"This is where we'll have our secret garden to go along with our treehouse," Harper said matter-of-factly.

Margaret smiled. "I love the imagination on you two. I have some extra seeds for you to use, but what about your garden on the farm? Do you still want that?"

"Oh, yes definitely," Abby confirmed. "We want to plant flowers here in the secret garden. We can play make-believe out here."

Margaret put her arms around the girls and ruffled their hair. "I have an idea. How about we add a little fairy woodland garden in your secret garden?"

"What do you mean, Mom?" Abby asked.

Margaret looked around the forested area before grabbing a few pretty rocks and lining them along the ground. "Well, we can make little fairy homes using rocks as pathways and stumps as little houses like this. The little fern shoots growing can be trees. I'm pretty sure the store down the street sells little fairy home knickknacks that you can add. It will be your little, secret world."

Harper squealed with excitement and hurried over to the creek, took her socks and shoes off, and let her feet dangle into the cold water, before Abby joined her.

"Our very own secret fairy garden. Dave, did you hear?" Harper yelled over to Dave.

Dave looked down from the tree house, which now had a very wide platform to stand on. "I did. I'm loving that idea. I think I'll get this tree house done by next week. Maybe we can have a tea party picnic in it?"

The girls clapped their hands in excitement and Margaret gazed up at Dave with a wide grin. "How's it coming along up there?"

Dave brushed his hands off on his jeans and jumped down onto the ground. "Well, I used up all of the boards I have and completed the bottom portion. I'll start the stairs and top next. I think I'm done for the day. I have to get to the beach house and get some work done there."

Margaret nodded. "Do you still want me to help out with the yard? The girls and I can come along."

Dave smiled. "I'd love that."

Margaret picked up her basket and called the girls over before walking out to the farm again where the sun shone brightly on the thriving garden plots.

"Can you believe how beautiful the farm looks? I have a feeling this year's crop is going to do a lot better than last year's," Margaret said, grabbing Dave's hand.

Dave stopped to admire the farm. "It's something. I'll tell you that. Want me to help you restock the farm stand before we leave?"

"That would be great."

Dave, Margaret, and the girls walked through the garden plots together, harvesting what was ready and filling another two baskets full before meeting at The Cape May Garden farm stand on the property with their bounties.

Margaret eyed the farm stand, noting a bunch of stuff had been taken, then picked up the money box.

"There's nothing in here. Not even a dollar. I know this farm stand was completely full of items two days ago," Margaret said, frustrated.

Dave sighed. "You're kidding."

Margaret slammed the money box shut. "So much for the honor system working."

Dave took the money box to look for himself. "I have a better solution for the money box that would make it harder to steal from."

Margaret took a deep breath and relaxed some. "Thank you, Dave. I'm hoping that this was just a one-time thing and that most people can be trusted. We just don't have the means to always have someone manning the stand at all times."

Dave eyed his truck. "How about we head over to the beach house and grab some lunch. Don't worry about the farm stand. I'll get the new money box in shortly."

"Sounds perfect," Margaret said as she wrangled the girls into the truck.

After an outdoor lunch at Barry's, their new favorite restaurant, they made their way down the block to Dave's house.

Dave got to work renovating the kitchen while Margaret hung out in the backyard with the girls. She looked around at the rocks covering every inch of the backyard. Surely, there was something better she could do with it, not to mention the rocks were painful to walk on.

The girls played while Margaret sketched out some ideas on the notepad she'd brought. Giddy with excitement, she looked over to the kitchen window to see Dave already caked in dust. She caught his eye and motioned for him to come out for some fresh air.

"I know that look. What ideas do you have swirling around?" Dave asked playfully.

"Well, I think we should do away with these rocks and add some lush green grass and some arborvitaes along the fence for extra privacy. Then, I was thinking some perennial flower beds —perfect for the monarch butterflies. Over here by the house, we would get rid of these old concrete steps and add in a beautiful brick patio with a table, chairs, and umbrella. We can add the white string market lights above the patio and have a fire pit in the back corner there."

Dave smiled. "I'm loving this so far. How about a horse-shoe pit off to the side there, too?"

Margaret nodded. "I like that. I was also thinking a little hut-like tiki bar in the corner would be fun. We could set up stools around it and maybe have a small TV in it to watch games or movies. Then, on the fence, we can add a white sheet for movie projector nights."

Dave sighed. "Gosh, you're really making me want to live here and not rent it out."

Margaret watched the girls happily play tag around the yard. "Have you decided what your plan is for this house?"

Dave shook his head. "I still haven't decided. I know it's going to cost some money to get this house in good shape. That part weighs on my mind—if I rent it out, it could help offset the costs; however, another part of me is ready to move off the wildlife refuge and be closer to the beach. Then again, moving off the refuge means I'll have a much longer commute to work, which wouldn't be *that* big of a deal, but still ...."

Margaret grabbed his hand. "Well, I'm sure whatever you decide will work out in the end."

Just then, Chris walked out into his backyard, looked over, and waved at them. "Hey, you two. How's it going?"

Dave raised his hand. "Oh, it's going. Just trying to decide what I'm going to do with this place."

Chris chuckled. "Well, I love good neighbors, and I'm all for you moving in. Have you by chance talked to Sarah today? I was trying to get ahold of her to let her know about a newly scheduled sunset tour tonight. I know she wanted to join in. It's been a few hours and I haven't heard back."

Margaret shook her head. "Nope, I haven't."

Chris said he'd see them later and walked back inside. Then Margaret's eyes widened. "Oh, no."

"What?" Dave asked.

"I just remembered something. I think Sarah's meeting up with Mark ... for the first time since they broke up."

Dave shook his head. "That doesn't sound good. Isn't she with Chris now?"

Margaret sighed. "Yes, she's with Chris. Mark kept calling, trying to get ahold of her. His mother died, and I guess he needs someone to talk to right now. Not to mention, I think she's having a hard time with Chris's ex calling constantly. She's in a weird place right now."

Dave shrugged. "I think who she really needs to talk to right now is Chris. She needs to let him know how she feels."

* * *

Sarah walked into the diner with her heart racing. It had been a few months since she'd last seen Mark, everything still felt so raw and fresh.

She was explaining to the hostess that she was meeting someone when Mark, already seated at a booth, spotted her and waved to get her attention. Sarah waved back and walked over. Mark stood to give her a hug, and Sarah awkwardly hugged him back.

"It's so good to see you," Mark said, eyeing her up and down.

Sarah sat down in the booth. "It's good to see you too, Mark."

Mark stared at her, smiling. "You look great. I mean it."

Sarah laughed. "Well, it's probably all of that summer sun."

They both looked the menu over. Sarah took a lot more time deciding than Mark since she was actually reading the offerings. Mark figured it didn't much matter what he ordered, he would rather look at her.

"I'm so sorry to hear about your mom, Mark. I know how close you two were," Sarah said as she placed her menu on the table.

Mark clasped his hands and looked for the waitress. "Geez, where is our waitress. I'm starving."

Sarah scrunched her brow. "Did you want to talk about your mom? That's why you wanted to meet, right? To have someone to talk to? I know it must be hard for you."

Just then, the waitress showed up. "You two ready to order? What'll it be?"

Sarah glanced at her menu again. "I'll have the BLT and an iced tea."

Mark, feeling relieved at the perfect timing of the waitress, took a deep breath. "I'm going to have the turkey club with a lemonade, please."

The waitress nodded, collected the menus, and carried on to the next table.

Mark tried to change the subject. "So, how's your coffee-house doing?"

Sarah suspected something was amiss. Mark was acting strangely and dodging questions about his mom, and it didn't sit right with her. "It's great, Mark. The Monarch is doing really well, thankfully. But enough about me, how are you holding up after your mom's passing?"

Mark rolled his eyes. "Look. My mom didn't really pass away. I said that so you would call me back and meet up with me. I was desperate."

Sarah's mouth dropped wide open. "Are you—? You *lied* about your mother's death to meet up with me? What is wrong with you?"

Mark dropped his face into his hands and shook his head. "You weren't calling me back. I needed to talk to you. The end of our relationship destroyed me. I needed one more chance to talk to you."

Sarah shook her head. "And you figured this is how to go about it?"

Mark looked out of the diner window. "Look, you broke up with me because of my job that had me traveling constantly. Well, guess what? I quit that job for you, and the new job I had lined up didn't work out. I'm jobless because of *you*."

Sarah's eyes widened. "Oh no. You do *not* get to blame me for being jobless. I didn't ask you to quit your job. Did you even think about asking your boss about traveling less or taking on a new position that would require less travel?"

Mark shook his head. "No. It was impulsive. I should have asked those questions. But you were my priority. I wanted you back any way that it took."

"Mark, you can't act like this. You lied to me about your mother, and now you're blaming me for being unemployed. How do you think that makes me feel? I'm starting to wonder why I even met up with you. Well, I know why—I felt sorry for you. I thought you needed a friend, and that maybe we *could* be friends."

Mark laughed "*Friends?* Friends? You think that's what I want? You've got to be kidding me."

Delivering their drinks, the waitress sensed the tension at the table, and her eyes cut back and forth between the two of them. "Your orders will be up shortly," she said uneasily.

Sarah, feeling uncomfortable, smiled at the waitress. "Great, can you bring the check when you bring our dishes? Thanks."

Mark scoffed. "The check? Why are you in such a hurry?"

"Mark, I have moved on. I thought coming here would be nice. I actually was hoping we could be friends, but I see that's not going to happen," Sarah said, as she swirled her straw around her drink.

"You've *moved on?* As in, you've found somebody else? Already? Like, I was just a blip in your radar? Was I that easy to get over? Everything we had meant nothing?"

Sarah's heart sank. "No, you were very hard to get over. I wanted something more than what you could give me, though. And yes, I'm with someone else."

Mark reached across the table and grabbed her hand, and Sarah immediately pulled it away as the waitress arrived with their sandwiches, setting them down on the table.

"OK, you two, here are your orders and your check. Let me know if you need anything else," the waitress said as she made a beeline back to the kitchen, presumably to get another table's order.

Sarah kept one hand in her lap and took a bite of her sandwich with the other.

Mark just sat there, his food untouched, watching her. "I want you to get back with me, Sarah. Let's give it another shot."

Sarah finished her bite before pulling her wallet out of her purse and putting a twenty on the table. "Mark, you are making me so uncomfortable with all of this. Frankly, even if I wasn't with someone else, I don't think I could date you again after how you lied to me about your mother then blamed me for the loss of your job."

Mark narrowed his eyes. "You're right. I don't know why I asked you to come here. You're not who I remember. You feel cold and shallow, not warm and inviting."

Sarah gathered her things and stood up from the table. "Well, enjoy the rest of your meal alone, Mark. I've had enough of this, and I regret even coming."

Mark forcefully grabbed Sarah's arm as she made her way out of the door. "Wait, Sarah, I'm sor—"

"Get off of me!" Sarah said in a loud voice as she pulled her arm away.

The entire diner turned to look, including Chris who had just walked inside to retrieve his takeout lunch before going to work.

Chris looked over from the host stand, and immediately ran to Sarah's aid. "Get your hands off of her. Who do you think you are?"

Mark, feeling embarrassed by the spectacle, threw cash down on the table for the bill and walked out of the diner abruptly.

Chris wrapped his arm around Sarah, grabbed his takeout from the host stand, left a few dollars tip in the jar, and walked outside. "Are you OK? What on earth happened in there? Who was that?"

Sarah wiped tears from her eyes. "It was my ex. The one I broke up with before you, but before you jump to conclusions, let me tell you why I was there." Sarah proceeded to tell Chris the entire story.

After hearing everything, Chris placed his takeout onto the ground, and wrapped his arms completely around Sarah, making her feel safer than she'd ever felt in her life. Sarah looked up at Chris and he wiped the tears from her cheeks with his hand and gave her a kiss.

Chris smiled, still embracing Sarah. "Well, while I have you here. I was trying to call earlier to ask if you wanted to join my sunset boat tour tonight. I figure you know enough about the birds to help educate the customers, and you would get some tips out of it, too."

Sarah laughed. "I would absolutely love that."

Just then, Chris's cell phone rang. He pulled his arms away from Sarah to take the call. "Give me one minute. I have to take this."

Sarah was sure that it was his ex again, but right now wasn't the time or place to discuss it. Too much had just happened at that diner, and it was the least of her worries at that moment.

* * *

Greg, Liz, and their sons, Steven and Michael, took a sunset walk around the farm, checking on the farm stand to make sure all money and produce was accounted for and looking over the beautiful vegetable, berry, and flower plants.

Greg ran his fingers over a tomato plant stem, then smelled his hands. "I absolutely love the way tomato plants smell. I don't know what it is. Maybe it's a bit of nostalgia and a bit of my love for tomatoes."

Liz nodded and reached down to look at the popsicle stick label in the ground. "It says Brandywine Heirloom. I think Dave and Margaret planted quite a bit of heirloom varieties out here."

Greg took a deep breath, closed his eyes, then popped them open again. "That's it. I think I've got the restaurant name. Heirloom."

Liz smiled. "Oh yeah? Heirloom?"

"Yep. We have so many dishes with tomatoes and I figure

we'll be using a lot of locally sourced heirloom tomatoes, probably even from this farm. I think it's fitting."

Liz wrapped her arms around Greg. "Heirloom. Heirloom. I like the sound of that. It definitely has a farm-fresh feel."

Greg kissed her on her head as they both turned to watch the boys kicking a soccer ball around. "I can't wait to get this restaurant open, not only to have patrons eat there, but to host my family and friends too."

CHAPTER TEN

The next day, while Donna was out with her mother, she received a phone call.

"Hello?"

"Hey. It's me, Dale."

Donna smiled and mouthed to her mom that she would catch up with her in the market and to go on ahead.

Dale cleared his throat since a bit of nerves had settled in. "What are you up to?"

Donna studied the produce in the market, her gaze landing on some withered, somewhat moldy strawberries. "Just looking around the market at the strawberries, which seem not very edible."

"Really? Well, I've got a place with the freshest strawberries around, and I happen to be in town dropping something off. Want to go with me?" Dale asked.

Donna laughed. "Well, I'm with my mom so I can't just up and leave right now. How about in an hour?"

"Perfect. I'll swing by and pick you up."

An hour later, Dale arrived, eager to go get strawberries. Energy and optimism emanated from him.

Donna hopped in the car, smiling at the excited man sitting next to her. "Wow, where are we going?"

Dale shifted the car into drive and looked over to smile at Donna. "You'll see."

Twenty minutes later, they pulled up to a farm full of endless rows of strawberries. The delicious-looking, bright-red berries popped among the green leaves of the plants. Families joyfully picked their bounties while taking photos of their little one's faces covered in smashed strawberries.

Donna squealed as they got out of the car and walked towards the farm. "Strawberry picking! I've been wanting to do this for years. It's literally been on my bucket list forever now."

Dale rubbed her back, walked up to the little cashier stand to pay, then grabbed an empty flat to fill with strawberries.

The hot sun warmed Donna's shoulders and her heart. This man was wooing her like no other man ever had, though the only other man had been Adam. She didn't have a Rolodex full of dates she could reference.

After picking strawberries for an hour, they walked back to the car with their huge harvest.

"That was so much fun, but what are we going to do with all of these?" Donna asked.

Dale thought for a moment. "Well, I'd say we could go back to my place, but I'm all the way in Collingswood. That's a good hour and a half or so. How about we drop them back to your parents' place, but after, we go somewhere else. Do you need to be anywhere?"

Donna shook her head. "Nope, I'm still job searching, so I have some free time."

Dale clapped his hands. "Perfect. Do you want to go kayaking on the bay?"

Donna's eyes lit up. "OK, but what makes you want to do all of these spontaneous things?"

Dale shrugged. "I don't know. I just really enjoy being with you, and I'm off today."

They drove to a kayak rental place on the bay and spent two hours kayaking, laughing, and enjoying themselves before heading back.

Upon parking in front of Donna's parents' house, Dale got out of the car first and grabbed the large flat of strawberries. "Can I bring them in for you? Will your parents mind?"

Donna smiled. "No, not at all. Come on in."

Dale made his way inside, carrying the strawberries, and immediately was drawn to Donna's dad's guitar collection in the corner of the dining room.

Donna took notice. "Oh, my dad is a guitar collector on top of being a musician."

Roy walked out from a back room and extended his hand. "Hello, there. I'm Roy, Donna's dad. And you are?"

Donna cut in. "Dad, this is my friend Dale. We picked these strawberries today and he wanted to help bring them inside."

Dale smiled and shook Roy's hand firmly.

Donna's mom came out of the kitchen. "Did I hear you picked strawberries? Oh, these would be perfect for making jam and smoothies. Here let me grab them for you. And you're Dale, I heard?"

Dale smiled. "That's me. Nice to meet you."

Dale looked back at the guitar collection. "Wow, that's some collection you've got there."

Roy nodded proudly. "Yep. It's my pride and joy. That one there is Donna's from when she used to play. I just tuned it up. Do you play?"

"I do. I hear Donna used to be an amazing player," Dale said enthusiastically while smiling at Donna.

Roy walked over and grabbed the guitars. "Here, you two. Come sit down and have at it. Show me what you know."

Donna sighed. "Dad, it's been so long. I'm afraid to find out that I've lost everything I've ever known."

Dale grabbed the guitar and strummed a few chords lightly

before looking over at Donna. "Start small with basics. Do you remember chords?"

Donna cleared her throat, and propped up her old guitar, before strumming a few chords shakily.

Dale smiled. "See. Look at what your mind retained. Now try this."

Donna and Dale both played simultaneously together, Donna remembering more and more as she played.

After about twenty minutes of warm-up exercises, Donna had very nearly remembered everything. She stood up with her guitar, closed her eyes, and played the most jaw dropping guitar solo, purely from memory.

Dale and Roy stopped what they were doing with shocked expressions on their faces.

"It's been over twenty years, and you just nailed that guitar solo like it was nothing. I'm truly awestruck," Dale said, feeling utterly smitten—more so than he'd ever felt with anyone.

Donna sat back down on the couch, hugging her guitar with tears in her eyes. "I can't believe how it all came back to me. I never knew if it would, and I've always been too afraid to find out."

Dale excitedly jumped up. "Look at you! You can do anything with that mind of yours."

Donna blushed and smiled, remembering how Adam never said much about her guitar playing or asked why she'd stopped. He'd always been too preoccupied with his own interests and career goals.

Donna looked over at Dale. "You know, you are one of the most positively influencing people I've ever met. You make people feel like they're capable of whatever their hearts desire. I admire that."

Dale's eyes sparkled as he looked over at Donna. "That has got to be the greatest compliment I've ever received. Thank you, Donna."

* * *

Later on that day, Greg stood on a ladder with Mike out front of the restaurant hanging the restaurant's sign.

Mike held the ladder and looked up at Greg. "So, Heirloom, it is, eh? I think I like it."

Greg groaned as he tried to reach the hook, eventually grabbing it and securing the sign. "Yep. Got the name idea while walking around the farm on our property."

Mike nodded, holding the ladder steady while Greg finished up and headed back down.

"Well, what do you think?" Greg asked, gazing up to admire the beautifully painted sign hanging above them.

Mike stepped back to get a better look. "Looks great, just needs to come up about five inches on the left side."

Greg cocked his head. "You're right. Spot me on the ladder again. I'm going back up."

Just then, Greg's dad, Ken, pulled up out front, and stepped out of the car. "My son! You're getting the sign up. You decided on Heirloom, eh?"

Greg nodded his head as he tried to balance the sign better from the ladder. "Yeah, Dad. That's the name. What do you think?"

Ken shrugged. "It's good, I guess. Have you figured out your chef situation yet?"

Mike piped in. "Actually, I'm the chef now. I'm Mike. Nice to meet you."

Ken extended his hand out to Mike. "You know what you're doing, I presume? I'm worried about my son. He needs someone good in that kitchen. He's never run a restaurant before."

Mike sighed while looking up at Greg. "I think I'm pretty good."

Greg came back down the ladder. "Dad, Mike is going to

do a great job. He's already proven himself with the dishes he's made from the menu already. I'm excited."

Ken walked towards the door. "Well, that's great. I'm going to go take a look around. I haven't seen the new updates yet."

"OK, we'll be in there in a minute, Dad," Greg said as he folded up the ladder.

Mike cleared his throat. "So, maybe now is a good time to tell you that I think we should ask Chef Ron if he would be interested in working alongside me, as a team."

Greg turned to look at Mike. "What are you talking about? You're perfectly capable. Are you worried you won't be able to do it? Because I have complete confidence in you."

Mike shook his head. "Thank you. I appreciate it. I just think the restaurant could benefit from two chefs who put their minds together. I'm starting to worry that it's going to be a lot on my plate, especially when I just found out I'm going to be a dad soon."

Greg smiled and gave a big back-pat hug to Mike. "Congratulations, Mike. That's wonderful. Though, I'm not sure Ron is going to want to work here again, let alone as the second chef, and will I be able to afford two chefs?"

Mike shrugged. "It can't hurt to ask. Maybe it could work somehow."

* * *

It was late afternoon, and Margaret and Liz decided to squeeze their obligatory beach day in, inviting Sarah and Donna along too.

They all sat in their chairs, enjoying the hot sun kissing their skin while watching the kids build sandcastles by the water.

Donna's face glowed with happiness and everyone noticed.

"What's gotten into you? You seem so refreshed and relaxed lately," Margaret asked.

Donna smiled and pushed her sunglasses off of her head and onto the bridge of her nose to cover her eyes. "Everything just feels wonderful since I went on that date with Dale."

Liz cleared her throat. "Really? Where exactly did he take you for your date?"

Sarah interrupted as she set some delicious looking items in front of them on the blanket. "Guys, come get some of these snacks. I made a little board of goodies. Homemade hummus, carrots, cucumbers, grapes, apples, cheese, and crackers."

Margaret's eyes widened. "OK, who brought the wine?"

Donna smiled, grabbing a bottle out of her backpack. "I've got you covered."

Liz made a plate and dipped her carrot into the hummus. "So, Donna, tell us about the date."

Donna took a sip from the glass of wine she'd just poured. "Well, he took me to a Phillies game. It was so much fun. Everything was perfect, down to the delicious hot dogs. We had great seats and great conversation. Then when the game ended, he asked me to go to his restaurant, Porridge, but here's where he really wooed me ..."

Liz rolled her eyes. "He stopped at a little florist shop and bought you a bouquet of sunflowers."

Donna furrowed her brow. "Yes! How did you know that? Did Dale tell Greg?"

Liz shook her head, while Margaret and Sarah sat on the edge of their seats. "Nope. Greg has been busy and hasn't talked to Dale since we were all on the beach together."

Sarah's eyes widened. "OK, now I need to know how you know."

Liz sighed. "Greg would kill me if he knew I've told you this, but I'm going to tell you because you're my friend."

Donna quickly grabbed a handful of grapes, and leaned forward in anticipation.

"Since Dale divorced and then had his heart broken from the following girlfriend, he became somewhat of a ... player, I guess you could say. I tried to tell you that when we were all together on the beach the other day, but I got interrupted," Liz said while watching her kids play in the sand.

Margaret, completely invested in where the story was going, spoke for Donna. "OK, so how does this relate to the sunflowers?"

Liz shook her head. "He plans out the same date with every woman he goes out with down to the T, and now I know he still does it because he did it with Donna."

"So, he stops and gets a bouquet of flowers for every girl? What's the big deal?" Donna asked.

Liz sighed. "It's not just the flowers. It's the Phillies game. It's the hot dogs. It's the stopping for flowers and going to Porridge afterwards. It may seem spontaneous on the date, but he literally does this with all the women—and there appears to have been a lot of them. I think you've been played."

Donna's stomach turned, and she sat back in her chair, feeling the giddy infatuation drain from her heart. "You're kidding. Why is he like that? He made me feel like we had something special."

Liz reached over and grabbed Donna's hand. "I'm sorry, but I had to tell you in case you were about to get hurt. Who knows … maybe he's changed. Maybe it was different with you."

Donna took a swig of wine. "I doubt it. I can't believe I introduced him to my parents. I feel so foolish."

"Your parents? When did that happen?" Sarah asked.

Donna sighed. "Yesterday. He asked me to go strawberry picking and kayaking, and afterwards he helped me bring the strawberries inside to my parents' place. He got to talking with my dad about guitars and everything. Was this another date he's used on countless women?"

Liz shook her head. "I've never heard of that one before."

Donna groaned and grabbed a huge chunk of cheese and popped it into her mouth. "I feel like my heart has just been torn to shreds. I haven't felt this way since Adam and I agreed on a divorce, and before that, in high school."

"Who broke your heart in high school if it wasn't Adam?" Margaret asked curiously.

Donna laughed. "Oddly, it was Dave."

Margaret furrowed her brow and pointed to herself. "Dave? As in my Dave?"

"Yep," Donna said matter-of-factly.

"What happened between you two?" Margaret asked.

Liz and Sarah watched and listened from their chairs, much like spectators at a tennis match.

Donna chuckled. "Nothing happened. That's exactly it. He was my brother's friend and I developed a huge crush on him. I went in for a kiss and he denied me. It would have been my first kiss and it took so much courage for me to do that. It destroyed me."

Margaret frowned. "I'm so sorry, Donna. That stinks."

Donna waved her hand as though it was nothing. "It was actually a good thing. I was feeling down in class the following day and Adam noticed. He came over to me during lab to see what was wrong, and thus sparked our romance. I know we're getting a divorce, but I did love Adam. He's a good man even if he's not good for me. Oddly, this whole thing with Dale is making me start to miss him."

Liz nodded. "What do you miss about him?"

Donna took a deep breath and looked out towards the ocean. "I don't know if it's specifically him I miss or just having someone. I guess I wasn't ready for the cruel reality of dating. I'm rusty with it all."

CHAPTER ELEVEN

It was another day of lounging and fishing at Corson's Inlet for Judy and Bob. The weather had turned hotter, and the crowds had picked up more in their little secluded area.

Judy sat in her chair under the umbrella beside Bob and looked at either end of the beach. Instead of being a good twenty-five feet apart, they were now about six feet from people on either side of them.

A chip bag rolled down the beach like a tumbleweed, smacking Judy in the arm before she grabbed it.

"This is ridiculous. This is the third piece of trash I've seen blow past us. It was never like this before," Judy said as she studied the bag.

Bob shook his head. "It is quite different when it's more crowded. I already stepped on a rusty fish hook someone left behind. Luckily it didn't pierce my skin. Here, I've started a little trash bag—toss it in there."

Judy thought for a moment. "I'm going to do a public service for this beach we love. I'm going to grab your little trash bag and collect what I find. I can't stand seeing the beach being treated like this. Who knows, maybe I'll find some shells along the way."

Bob nodded and checked his fishing line after seeing a small bite.

After setting off, Judy quickly came upon some empty soda bottles sitting near the dunes. She shook her head and immediately stuffed them into the bag.

Suddenly, two dogs raced towards her. Judy kneeled down and they stopped right in front of her, licking her face and hands.

Judy noticed the dogs had leashes attached to their collars and grabbed them. "My oh my. Who do you two belong to? You probably shouldn't be racing around by yourselves out here."

A man walked by and Judy caught his attention.

"Sir, are these your dogs?"

The man shook his head and continued on. Judy passed many more people, and not getting any affirmative responses about the dogs belonging to them, Judy continued to walk with them as she picked up one piece of trash after another until her bag was chock-full.

A woman came barreling down the beach holding her arms out towards the dogs. "Ziggy! Duke! There you are. I've been worried sick."

Judy smiled, not realizing who the woman was initially.

The woman looked Judy up and down as she grabbed the dog's leashes from her. "Oh, it's you. Well, thank you for grabbing them. I fell asleep on my chair over there and had tied their leashes to the arm rest. I guess they got loose. I was worried sick."

Judy gave each dog a head scratch. "Well, you have them back safe and sound."

The woman looked at Judy's overstuffed bag. "What's in the bag? Shells?"

Judy sighed. "No, it's full of litter. I was getting fed up with it all over the beach. I definitely see why you were a little wary of more people being on the beach you love."

The woman smiled and extended her hand. "We've never formally met. I'm Darla. And you are?"

Judy shook her hand. "I'm Judy. We're sitting way over there—me and my husband, Bob. That's where I found your dogs. We've really been enjoying coming here."

Darla looked in the direction that Judy said she was set up at. "Well, it was nice to meet you. I apologize for how I acted before. I guess you can see why I can be how I am. However, someone like you, I'm happy to share this beach and shells with. I've got a little something I want to give you. Give me a second."

Darla walked back to her blanket with the dogs before returning with a bag. "Here. This is for you."

Judy's eyes widened as she looked inside. "A bag full of sea glass in all colors. Are you kidding? How long did it take you to find all of this?"

Darla laughed as her dogs barked at a bird flying by. "A few years. I brought it to the beach today to make some sand art with it. I kind of wanted to give it back to Mother Nature. However, I think I want you to have it, especially after the way I treated you."

Judy closed the bag and smiled, looking at the two dogs enjoying themselves as they talked. "I will treasure this always. I have many ideas for crafting with it, and honestly, I'm probably going to start tonight. Though, how about we each take a handful and design a little something in the sand here, like you initially wanted to do. It's pretty exciting to think about all the people who will be surprised to see it."

Just then, a man walked up to Darla and gave her a kiss on the cheek. "Hi. Whatcha up to?"

Darla handed the dog leashes to the man and gave him a hug. "This is Judy. Judy, this is my husband, Joel."

Joel shook Judy's hand. "Nice to meet you. I hope Darla's not giving you any trouble. She's quite protective of *her* beach," he said with a chuckle.

Darla nudged him in the ribs. "OK, I'll meet you at the chairs in a bit, dear. We're going to make some art in the sand now."

Joel chuckled some more and walked back to the chairs with the dogs.

As Judy and Darla grabbed handfuls of the sea glass, a lightbulb went off in Judy's head. She picked out some larger brown sea glass pieces and staggered many of them leading towards the ocean. She added green pieces for the head, arms, and legs on each brown piece.

Darla stopped what she was doing to marvel. "They look just like baby sea turtles making their way to the ocean. That is incredible."

A bunch of passersby stopped to look and take photos.

Judy smiled proudly.

Darla finished her design and stood back to look at it with Judy.

"Keep me trash free," Judy read aloud.

Darla put her hand on her hip and nodded. "It's fitting for the sea turtles and the rest of the sea life and fauna that are affected by the trash."

More people walked by, snapping photos, and admiring the beautiful sea glass detail and message.

Darla took a deep breath of fresh salt air. "I think I found my new calling."

Judy paused. "What's that?"

Darla looked around at her favorite place. "Keeping this beach as trash free as possible, and educating others to do the same. You've inspired me, Judy. Instead of harboring annoyance with others on this beach, I'm going to share my love of this beautiful place with them and inspire others to take action to keep it beautiful and clean. Maybe I'll even share my beach finds with them," she said with a wink.

* * *

Sarah wrapped her arms around Chris and leaned her head affectionately on his shoulder as he methodically steered the boat around the bay at sunset.

Chris pulled up to a secluded spot by the marsh full of the shorebirds they loved to watch. He let the engine come to a full stop, kissed the top of Sarah's head, and walked with her to the front railing.

Sarah pulled out her binoculars—her own pair that Chris had given her—and sharpened the focus to get a better look.

Chris stood behind her and, since he was almost a foot taller than her, gazed over her with his binoculars. "Look at those black skimmers. The way they fly low enough to skim the water with their beaks open to catch fish always fascinates me. I think they've got to be my favorite shorebird."

Sarah moved her binoculars to see the skimmers in action, just as one caught a fish and shut its beak. "Wow, it just got one. I could watch them all day."

Chris leaned his body on the railing to face Sarah. "You know, part of what I love about this job is that I get to educate people about these beautiful creatures. Some of them are a threatened species, and I think it's important for people to be knowledgeable of them and their habitats."

Sarah lowered her binoculars and leaned against the adjacent railing, smiling at Chris. "I love that about you. You have such an appreciation for beautiful things in this world and try to make their existence known and protected."

Chris smiled, reached over, and pushed a stray hair off of Sarah's face just as his phone rang. Sarah grabbed his hand, hoping to stop him from answering his phone and interrupting their special moment.

Chris held his finger up, and started walking to the back of the boat for privacy. "Give me one minute. I have to take this."

Sarah's heart dropped in her chest. It had to be his ex, *again*. Today had been one of the first days they'd been together where she hadn't called at all, that is until now.

Five minutes later, Chris walked back, a smile forming on his face again. "Sorry about that. Where were we?"

Sarah had her back turned to him as she looked out towards the marsh and didn't turn around when he came back.

"Hey, you. What do you see out there?" Chris asked, trying to get her attention again.

Sarah abruptly turned back towards him. "What do I see? I see someone who can't set boundaries with his ex. I thought we'd finally gotten a day together without being interrupted by her, but that was short-lived."

Chris hung his head. "It wasn't my ex this time, but I get it. She does call a lot. I—"

Sarah cut in. "Chris, I understand she's your son's mother, but there is no reason for her to call five times a day or more. You can't put up with that, and frankly, I don't know if it's something I could live with."

Chris looked at Sarah, the sunset casting a warm glow over his face. "I told her the other day that she can't call me all of the time anymore. We had a long talk, and in the end, she understood. It was kind of a hard conversation to have, honestly. I've wanted to do it for a long time now. I think she's had a hard time with being a single mother and her family living across the country. The good news is she's met someone, and he sounds great. I'm quite relieved and happy about it. Sam seems to love him too."

Sarah took a deep breath and blew it, feeling a ton of tension release off of her shoulders. "Really? I'm so glad to hear that. I've been wanting to talk to you about it, but didn't feel it was my place, being that we haven't been dating for very long."

Chris wrapped his arms around Sarah, pulling her in close. "I'd like to date a lot longer."

Sarah nestled her head into his chest. "I'm feeling that too."

Chris's phone rang again, this time he clicked the silent button without even looking at it.

Sarah furrowed her brow. "Aren't you going to answer it?"

Chris shook his head. "Nope. I'm pretty sure I know who it is, and I'll call them back."

Sarah smiled. "Who called earlier if it wasn't your ex, if you don't mind me asking?"

Chris shrugged. "It's a surprise. You'll find out soon enough. My lips are sealed for now."

Sarah felt giddy excitement. Her birthday was tomorrow, and maybe, just maybe, he remembered that when she'd told him on their first date.

* * *

Meanwhile across town, Donna looked at her phone as Dale called, debating whether she wanted to talk to him. She still couldn't shake her anger that he'd treated her like every other woman he'd courted on identical dates.

Donna reluctantly answered her phone. "Hello?"

"Hey there, good looking. How are you?" Dale asked playfully.

Donna rolled her eyes. "I'm fine. How are you, Dale?"

Loud, bustling kitchen noises could be heard in the background. "I'm good. I'm at work. We're closing early since a private party never showed, and I was wondering if you wanted to stop by for some dinner on the house?"

Donna clenched her teeth, ready to give him grief, but gave it a second thought. "OK. I can do that. What time?"

Dale looked at the clock. "How about six thirty?"

Donna smirked. "Great. That will give me time to pick up a few things."

Dale smiled. "See you then."

Donna quickly got dressed, and drove towards the restaurant, making a couple of stops along the way.

Once at the restaurant, she flung the door open and walked in with determination.

Dale walked out of the kitchen to greet her with open arms. "Hey, you—"

Donna pulled a bouquet of sunflowers and two hot dogs from behind her back and threw them into Dale's arms. "I hear you like to play women with the same exact date down to the sunflowers and hot dogs. I thought you'd be needing these for your next date." She spun, storming off towards the door.

Dale quickly set the items on the counter. "Donna, wait. It's not like that."

Donna abruptly turned around, full of anger and heartache. "It's not like what? I don't want to be a part of your little game, Dale. I have only been with one man in my entire life. I don't understand this dating game you have going on here. Here I thought we had something really special, but it turns out it's not special at all because you do it with every woman you take out. And I hear there's a lot of them."

Dale shook his head. "Donna, please let me explain."

Donna flicked her hand in the air, and stormed out of the door this time, making her way to her car and driving back towards Cape May with the windows down and the music blaring, adrenaline pumping through her veins.

Her phone rang a few times, and when she saw it was Dale, she turned it off. She had never felt so good and so awful at the same time. She never knew she had that in her, to be able to stand up for herself like *that*.

Her favorite song came on the radio, and she turned it up, singing along loudly as the wind whipped her hair in every direction.

An hour and a half later, she arrived back to her parents', said hello, and immediately retreated to her room, crashing on her bed.

Did that really just happen? Donna thought to herself. It took her a while to slowly wind down and drift off to sleep.

A knock came at her door, waking her up. "Donna, dear. You have a visitor," her mom said through the door.

"A visitor? Who?" Donna asked, confused.

Donna's mom chuckled. "Just look out front."

Donna walked towards the front door and peeked out the window. "Mom, I don't see anyone. What are you talking about?"

Donna's dad looked over from his recliner and loud TV show. "He knocked on the door and asked for you. It took a minute for your mom to wake you. Maybe he left."

Donna opened the door and walked outside in bare feet, looking around the front yard.

Just then she saw someone playing guitar on the front curb under the street light.

Dale looked over to see her, standing up from the curb, and walking towards her while still playing the guitar.

Dale looked Donna in the eyes. "I learned your solo that you played the other day. Do you recognize it?"

Donna shrugged. "Yes, I guess. What are you doing here, Dale?"

Dale sighed and stopped playing for a moment. "Yes, I admit I have taken other women on that Phillies date."

Donna interjected. "You mean *many* other women."

Dale rolled his eyes, sighing. "Only one of those women went strawberry picking and kayaking with me. That date was genuine because I like you. I *really* like you. I want you to know that you *are* special to me. I was going through a heartbreak phase after my last relationship. It tore me up, and I thought throwing myself into the dating scene would heal me faster. It didn't. I didn't feel a connection with any of them, but I do with you. I could barely pay attention to the baseball game because I was so enthralled with you."

Donna put her hand on her face, feeling slight embarrassment and relief. "Really? You're not just telling me this?"

Dale laughed and gently pulled her hand off of her face.

"Would I drive an hour and half to chase down a woman I didn't care for? Look at you, you're beautiful."

Donna blushed. "So, what now?"

Dale strummed his guitar. "Well, do you like me? Do *you* feel a connection?"

Donna rocked back on her bare feet on the grass. "Yes. Yes, I do."

Dale strummed his guitar again. "Well, let's see where it takes us. No pressure. No expectations. Just you and me figuring out what love is."

Donna smiled. "I like that, but you'd better give me that guitar so I can show you how it should be played."

CHAPTER TWELVE

A few days later, Greg and Mike went on a search for Chef Ron early in the morning.

"Are you sure this is the place?" Greg asked.

Mike nodded as he looked at the ramshackle restaurant made from an old train caboose. "I'm told this is where he's working now. I hear he does the breakfast shift."

Greg sighed. "Since he's not taking our calls, I guess it's come to this. Shall we go inside?"

Mike hopped out of the car, shutting the door behind him. "Why not. I'm hungry anyway."

Greg followed him inside the little old restaurant where they were seated at a small table in the back adorned with a vase of silk flowers. An old jukebox played doo-wop music, and a lot of yelling and noise came from the kitchen.

"OK, so why don't we order some food, and then try and talk to Ron," Greg said as he looked over the menu.

An older waitress with a raspy voice who smelled like cigarettes came over. She pulled her notepad out of her apron. "Welcome to Olga's. What can I get you?" she asked without any enthusiasm at all.

Mike spoke up first. "I'll have two eggs over easy, home fries, and scrapple. Rye toast is fine and coffee as well.

"And I'll have the cream-chipped beef. Coffee is fine for me too. By the way, does someone named Ron work in the back?" Greg asked as he handed their menus to the waitress.

The waitress thought for a moment. "I think so. He may be that new guy back there. Did you want me to tell him to come out?"

Greg nodded. "That'd be great. Thanks."

A few minutes later, Ron came out holding his kitchen apron in his hand. "What are you two doing here?"

"You haven't been returning our calls, and we wanted to talk to you," Greg answered.

Ron sighed and pulled up a chair to the table. "Look, I ruined a good thing at your place, and I was embarrassed. My life is in shambles and I had to take the first job that was offered to me to make ends meet right now."

Mike looked around the restaurant. "Are you the chef here?"

Ron looked down at the floor. "Nope. I took a demotion to get work quickly. I'm a line cook."

Just then, a guy popped his head out of the kitchen. "Ron! What are you doing sitting out there? We need you in the kitchen. That's what we pay you for, after all. And the omelet you just made was wrong. We don't do caprese omelets here. They simply wanted an American cheese and tomato omelet, not one with mozzarella and basil."

Ron shook his head. "I'll be right back in."

Greg looked over at the guy in the kitchen who was still staring at Ron from the kitchen window. "Do you like working here?"

Ron laughed. "Not at all. I'm treated like crap. The food is terrible. They use that super-processed cheese that's individually wrapped and frozen vegetables here. It's terrible. I was trying to make something that was actually edible."

Mike chuckled. "Well, now maybe you see how we felt working under you at the restaurant. You pretty much acted like that guy who just yelled at you."

Ron sighed. "I'm starting to see what a jerk I was. I guess I literally had to be put in the shoes of those who worked under me to truly understand. Why didn't anyone ever say anything to me?"

Greg shrugged. "We tried. Look, Ron, we have an offer for you—"

Mike interrupted. "We want you to be a chef alongside me at Heirloom."

Ron smiled. "Is that what you're calling the restaurant? I like it. I don't think two chefs is going to work out, though. Mike, you deserve the role as chef and you should own it."

Mike rolled his eyes. "This was *my* idea. I want you to be a chef alongside me. I think we would make a great team and Greg agrees. Plus, it's got to be better than what you've got going here."

Ron smiled, relief settling inside him. "When can I start?"

"Whenever you can," Greg said, eyeing the waitress who approached with their dishes.

Ron stood up from the table, letting the waitress serve them. "How about tomorrow?"

Greg furrowed his brow. "Are you sure? You don't have to square things away here first?"

Ron laughed and watched the waitress walk back to the kitchen out of earshot. "I'm not going to last much longer here. It's wearing down on what little spirit and creativity I have left. Not to mention, I can't work under that guy in the back. I promise to never act like him again, trust me. If you're serious, I'm going to finish my shift and be done today. I don't care about burning bridges here. It's a toxic environment."

Greg and Mike shook Ron's hand in agreement before he turned back to the kitchen.

Greg took a sip of his coffee. "Oh yeah. My friend Dale

who owns Porridge in Collingswood offered to mentor you for a couple of weeks at his restaurant. It wouldn't be every day due to the drive, but maybe a few days a week? Would you be interested? Maybe gain a little more insight and training before we open?"

Mike took a bite of scrapple. "Are you kidding me? I would love that. Does he know that Ron is coming back, though?"

Greg smirked. "Actually, I told him last night about everything that happened, and he thinks second chances are sometimes important."

* * *

Racing against the sunset, Margaret, Liz, Dave, Greg, Donna, and Chris hurried around the beach setting up chairs, blankets, food and drinks, and beach games.

"What time is she supposed to get here, Chris?" Margaret asked as she opened the tops off the dips under the canopy away from the seagulls.

Chris looked at his watch. "Any minute now. Why don't you all stand in the canopy so she doesn't see you when she walks down."

Everyone except Chris hurried under the canopy, awaiting Sarah's arrival.

Minutes later, Sarah walked onto the beach and over to Chris, giving him a hug. "Hey, you."

Chris hugged her back. "Happy birthday, Sarah. I thought we could meet here for some beach time together."

Everyone under the canopy couldn't contain their excitement and burst out.

"Happy birthday, Sarah!" they yelled.

Sarah almost fell backwards from the surprise. "You guys! I can't believe this. I had no idea you were under that canopy."

Chris laughed. "This is our little birthday setup for you. There's food and drinks under the canopy."

Sarah nudged Chris playfully. "Did you set all of this up yourself?"

Chris nodded proudly. "Remember when I took that call on the beach? It wasn't my ex. It was from the caterer. That call on the boat? That was Margaret helping me set this up. I had to be discreet. It was so hard keeping this a secret from you."

Sarah threw her hand over her mouth. "Oh my goodness, and this whole time I was annoyed with you over it. I feel terrible."

Chris put his arm around her waist. "Don't be silly. Go out and spend time with your friends. They're going to eat all of those delicious dips up if you don't get over there."

Sarah laughed, making her way to the group but not before turning towards Chris again. "Wait. Did you say caterer?"

Chris nodded. "Yep. You'll find out later."

After a couple hours of hanging on the beach, enjoying the sunset, and gabbing with each other, Chris stood up to make an announcement. "OK, we should probably all pack up and head back to my place. We've got more celebrating to do."

Working together to take everything down, the group then headed across the street to Chris's where beautiful white string market lights had been strung across the entire backyard. A caterer was finishing putting the food out on a couple of tables in the backyard as Dale oversaw the process.

Donna stepped through the gate into the backyard and immediately locked eyes with Dale across the yard.

Liz nudged her playfully. "I guess that's the other surprise. We all knew Dale was going to be here helping the caterer, but just so *happened* to forget to tell you."

Dale walked right up to Donna. "I heard you were going to be here. I'm glad. I couldn't wait to see you again, especially after the other night."

Donna gently touched his hand. "I'm glad to see you too."

Moments later, Chris turned off the music and white string lights, cueing everyone of what was to come.

One by one, the friends lit sparklers, all except Dale and Donna.

"Are you ready?" Dale asked Donna.

"Ready for what?" Donna chuckled.

"Let's go sing and play for the birthday girl. I've got two guitars just waiting for us by the tree."

Dale looked over at Chris and nodded as he grabbed Donna's hand and led her to the guitars.

"I don't know if I remember the chords for the song." Donna said as she lifted the guitar.

Dale smiled. "You will. Just follow my lead."

And just like that, the dark, starry night sky was lit by brightly colored sparklers, and Dale and Donna sang and played for Sarah while Chris walked out with the most beautiful cake lit up with candles.

Sarah blew out the candles with closed eyes, wishing for something she truly wanted and knew she was well on her way to getting.

EPILOGUE

July was fast approaching, and Dave had sped up his beach house renovation exponentially with the help of friends. Not to mention, Margaret was about done with the final touches on the yard.

Dave called for Margaret from the backyard. "Hey, you. I think we're ready."

Margaret's eyes widened. "Really? You think?"

Dave nodded. "Yep. I just finished putting the shelves up. This house is about finished. It's time to finally show it off."

Margaret pulled out her phone and texted her local friends and family. She and Dave had been so excited about the final reveal after all of their hard work. Margaret had also helped out with sanding, painting, and numerous other tasks inside the home, so it definitely was a team effort.

Margaret walked inside the house, but not before turning to look back at the yard one last time. She brimmed with excitement over what they'd created. They made such a great team when it came to projects, as evidenced by the farm, The Cape May Garden stand, and The Seahorse Inn.

About a half hour later, they waited out front as their friends and family pulled up to see the house on short notice.

Already, the changes just from the front of the house were evident at first glance. It had been painted a beautiful tan-taupe color with a white and ocean-blue trim, a decided upgrade from the old, chipped gray paint.

Margaret led the final walk-through with Dave trailing in the back behind everyone, delighting in their reactions. "And this is the front porch. You should have seen it before."

Judy and Bob gawked. "Wow, it's absolutely gorgeous. Is this hardwood new?"

Dave chimed in, "Yes. Believe it or not, it used to be old, faded Astroturf. I put in new screens, and Margaret picked out this beautiful porch furniture for relaxing during sunset."

Chris and Sarah walked into the house from the porch first. "My man. This is absolutely stunning. I wish my house next door looked this nice."

Liz and Greg went to check out the bathroom. "A floor-to-ceiling tile shower? This is what I want at our house, Greg."

Donna and Dale meandered around the new kitchen, eyeing the new stainless steel appliances, apron sink, and granite counter-tops. Above the new island hung three star-shaped light fixtures.

The kids ran out towards the backyard while everyone followed. The rocks were gone, replaced with soft, fuzzy green sod. Margaret had added the same string lights that Chris had in his backyard, along with a freshly laid brick patio, and multiple low-maintenance perennial flower beds.

Dave stood behind Margaret, his arms around her, while propping his chin on top of her head. "This place came together so perfectly."

Margaret watched as their friends and family stopped to look at different things around the yard. "Have you figured out what you're going to do with this beach house? I know you go back and forth."

Dave looked over at Chris, who was tossing a football to the kids. "I was pretty sure that I was going to rent it out, but I think I'm going to move in for the summer at the very least. The house is beautiful, right across the beach, and has great neighbors. Well, at least Chris is a great neighbor. I haven't met the people on the other side yet, though Chris tells me they mainly rent their house out for the summer."

Margaret smiled. "Yeah, I can see why you'd want to move in. It has everything going for it."

Dave thought for a moment. "You know, I love my job over at Pinetree Wildlife Refuge and living on the property, but I think I'm ready for a change. This is the first property I've owned since the divorce. It feels pretty good."

Harper and Abby came running up to them out of breath. "OK, we're starving. Can we order pizza?"

Margaret laughed. "Sure, in a little bit. Go play with your cousins some more. Look, they're already looking to see where you went."

Meanwhile, across the yard, all of the adults had gotten cozy sitting in the Adirondack chairs around the firepit.

Chris pulled his chair closer to Sarah's, grabbing her hand and intertwining his fingers with hers.

Sarah looked at him, smiled, and looked back at the fire. "I love it here. I love everything they did. I need to get myself a beach house someday."

Chris looked back over at his house. "Why don't you ... move in with me?"

Sarah abruptly turned to him "What?"

Chris fumbled on his words, nervous over his bold statement even though he'd daydreamed about for a while. "I know it sounds way too soon, but I'm sick of societal timelines and deadlines. We get along like peas in a pod, and frankly, I'm ready to take the next step if you are."

Sarah was shocked. She had not expected Chris to ask her to move in *at all.* "How will that work? I have my place already. Will it be weird with your son having me live there so soon?

Will it be too soon for our relationship? I don't want to ruin a good thing too fast."

Chris rubbed her hand. "Sam loves you, and plus, I only see him on the weekends and a couple week nights. His mom has him during the week so it gets pretty lonely here. You're renting your place, right? Come save money and live with me. If we're meant to be, it will only strengthen us, right? I don't know about you, but I'm ready to find out sooner than later if we're going to be together until we're old and gray. This seems like a good first step."

Sarah squeezed his hand and winked. "Well, my lease is month-to-month, but let me sleep on it."

* * *

Pick up **Book 5** in the Cape May Series**, Cape May Summer Nights,** to follow Margaret, Liz, the rest of the familiar bunch, and some new characters.

Follow me on Facebook at **https://www. facebook.com/ClaudiaVanceBooks**

ABOUT THE AUTHOR

Claudia Vance is a writer of women's fiction and clean romance. She writes feel good reads that take you to places you'd like to visit with characters you'd want to get to know.

She lives with her boyfriend and 2 cats in a charming small town in New Jersey, not too far from the beautiful beach town of Cape May. She worked behind the scenes on tv shows and film sets for many years, and she's an avid gardener and nature lover.

CPSIA information can be obtained
at www.ICGtesting.com
Printed in the USA
BVHW031200140122
626220BV00013B/113